"I guess I'm destined to spend the rest of my life alone." Libby sobbed harder.

"Libby, no." Heath hugged her close. "That's not true. And as for Liam not finding you desirable, well..." He gripped her shoulders and nudged her back just far enough to meet his gaze. "He's a fool, because I think you're adorable."

"You do?" She sniffled, peering up at him with her pretty blue eyes.

"Of course. You're sweet and funny and thoughtful. Any guy in his right mind would think you're a serious catch."

"Really?"

He nodded, intoxicated by her sweet smell— strawberries and snapdragons and summer night air all rolled into one.

"B-because I think you'd be a good catch, too." He couldn't fully focus on her words, because as she spoke, she drifted closer and closer until her warm breath tickled his lips. Lips that had been so long without comfort or warmth they'd forgotten the simple pleasure of pressing against another's.

She leaned closer.

And so did he.

Dear Reader,

Have you ever been at a party where you didn't know anyone? Or maybe you did know people, but didn't really feel you belonged? That sensation is the *worst!*

Sometimes when I'm at a big writers' conference, I find myself lost in a sea of strangers. It makes me feel lonely and a little scared. I know I should use the opportunity to make new friends, but that's not always easy. Every once in a while, a kind soul wanders up to spark a conversation, and that lone sweet gesture changes everything.

When this story opens, Libby Dewitt's lost in not just a crowd, but seemingly, the whole world. She's *very* pregnant, estranged from her baby's father and even her parents. When her car, finances and health also let her down, she's forced to rely on the kindness of strangers, and she finds herself immersed in the kind of wondrous family she'd never dreamed possible.

Trouble is, her new life is an illusion. And her inevitable leaving will open old wounds. Making matters worse is the man whose mere presence gives her glimpses into the life she's always wanted, but fears may never be.

Will Libby make Heath Stone believe in second chances? Or is she destined to raise her baby alone? I'll never tell! Lol!

Happy reading!

Laura Marie

THE SEAL'S BABY

—

LAURA MARIE ALTOM

HARLEQUIN® AMERICAN ROMANCE®

Recycling programs
for this product may
not exist in your area.

ISBN-13: 978-0-373-75524-0

THE SEAL'S BABY

Copyright © 2014 by Laura Marie Altom

Printed in U.S.A.

HARLEQUIN®
www.Harlequin.com

ABOUT THE AUTHOR

After college (Go, Hogs!), bestselling, award-winning author Laura Marie Altom did a brief stint as an interior designer before becoming a stay-at-home mom to boy-girl twins and a bonus son. Always an avid romance reader, she knew it was time to try her hand at writing when she found herself replotting the afternoon soaps.

When not immersed in her next story, Laura teaches art at a local middle school. In her free time, she beats her kids at video games, tackles Mount Laundry and, of course, reads romance!

Laura loves hearing from readers at either P.O. Box 2074, Tulsa, OK 74101, or by email, balipalm@aol.com.

Love winning fun stuff? Check out www.lauramariealtom.com.

Books by Laura Marie Altom

HARLEQUIN AMERICAN ROMANCE

For my dear old friend and talented author, Amy Lillard.

Have I mentioned lately how blessed I feel to have you back in my life?!

Chapter One

"Sam? Where the hell are you?" Southern Oregon's dense coastal fog absorbed Heath Stone's words, rendering his words useless in the search for his dog, who lately felt like his only friend.

Heath had let him out the previous night at 2200 for his usual evening constitutional, but the dog had caught the scent of something, and a chase ensued through the forest thick with sitka spruce, western hemlock and red cedar. Heath had spent the entire night searching the pungent woods, his footfalls silent on winding pine needle-strewn paths, all the while fighting the urge to panic.

Now, in dawn's fragile light, with his heart empty from mourning Patricia and the pain still too raw, he couldn't even consider suffering another loss. "Come on, Sam! Quit fooling around!"

Heath clapped, then whistled, hoping the shrill sound carried.

It did not.

Thirty minutes later, he'd wound his way back to the one-bedroom log cabin that for the past year he'd called home. After relieving himself, he washed his hands and splashed cold water on his face.

He took an energy bar from the cabinet alongside the

propane stove and a bottled water from the fridge. Stopping only long enough to retrieve his wallet and keys from the metal bucket he stored them in beside the door, he soon sat behind the wheel of the 1960 Ford pickup that his grandpa had bought new.

The trek down the cabin's single-lane drive proved daunting, with visibility being a few feet at best. After rolling down both windows, he called periodically out either side.

By the time he reached the main road, the fog had thinned to the point he could at least make out the double yellow lines on the pavement. Usually, at this time of the morning, he and Sam set out to fish on the Umpqua River. Most weekdays, the road was deserted. Hell, most weekends—unless his hometown of Bent Road was hosting a holiday festival or fishing tourney. Most tourists traveling north from Coos Bay on Oregon Coast Highway 101 blew right by the lonely road leading to the largely forgotten town. With no trendy B and Bs or campgrounds, visitors had no reason beyond curiosity to ever stop by. A fact that suited Heath just fine.

"Sam! You out there, boy?" Crawling along at the harrowing rate of fifteen miles per hour, Heath continued calling, intermittently scanning the faded blacktop for the potentially gut-wrenching sight of his wounded—or even dead—dog.

"What the—" He'd driven maybe five miles before pumping his brakes, having damn near hit not his dog, but a woman—a *very* pregnant woman—standing in the road's center, waving her arms. "What's the matter with you?" he hollered, easing the truck onto the weed-choked shoulder. "Got some kind of death wish?"

Upon killing the engine, he hopped out and slammed

the door shut behind him. The dense fog stole the thunder of a gratifying bang, leaving him with a less satisfactory thud.

"Th-thank you so much for stopping." The ethereal blonde staggered his direction. Was she drunk? "M-my car broke down yesterday. I tried walking, but—"

"It's a good thirty miles to town."

She placed her hands protectively over her bulging belly. "If you could just take me to a phone, I'd…" Before finishing her halting sentence, she crumpled before him like a building that had suddenly lost its foundation.

He rushed to her, checking her pulse and finding it strong.

Abandoning his worries for Sam, he hefted the woman's deadweight into his arms and then onto his truck's passenger seat.

He then retrieved her giant purse from the road.

"W-what happened?" she asked, stirring when he buckled her in and set her purse beside her.

"You fainted. How long has it been since you've had a decent meal?"

"I—I don't know. I'm saving my cash for gas."

The fog had lifted enough to reveal a VW Bug as old as his truck. The backseat was crammed so tightly with the woman's belongings, daylight couldn't even be seen through the front window.

"I'll run you to my cabin—get you fed and call for a tow."

"Thank you—but I don't have the money for a tow or mechanic."

He closed her door. "You prefer I leave you out here for the crows?"

Groaning, she pressed her fingertips to her forehead.

"What I'd prefer is to have never wound up in this position."

All too well, he knew the feeling.

LIBBY DEWITT STRUGGLED to stay awake while the stranger drove. Exhaustion—physical and emotional—weighed down her shoulders, making even turning her head an effort.

"Stay with me…" the man urged. "Sure I shouldn't take you straight to a doc?"

"I'm fine," she assured. It took much of her remaining energy to meet his curiously hollow stare. "Just tired and hungry."

"I can help with both of those issues. And since you're low on cash, I'll see what I can do with your car. But fair warning, I'm good with a lot of things, but engine repair has never been one of them."

From somewhere inside she managed a laugh. "At this point, a cracker and glass of water would be downright gourmet. To expect more would be greedy."

His sideways glance spoke volumes, but at the same time, nothing at all. Again, she had the sense that part of him was emotionally missing. What had he been through?

He turned the truck onto a dirt lane so narrow the weeds grew between twin tire ruts.

Woods, dark and brooding, surrounded them, yet over a small hill, sunbeams punched through the fog, the soft light promising to end the day's gloom.

Over the next hill stood the sweetest log cabin—sun- and weather-faded with rich green moss growing between the logs' seams. Two smallish paned windows flanked a wooden front door. A wide, covered porch held two rockers and a pair of dead hanging ferns. The Pacific glistened in teasing strips just beyond massive pines.

"I-it's beautiful," she said, not trying to disguise her awe. "How lucky you are."

Parking the truck, he shrugged. "It's okay."

Okay? To be jaded about such a view implied he wasn't really alive at all. Despite the lousy circumstances she found herself in, Libby hoped she'd never lose her ability to be wowed by Mother Nature showing off.

"You able to walk under your own steam?"

"I—I think so…" To prove it she opened the door with an echoing creak, then placed her feet firmly on the ground. Her legs wobbled a little at first, but then held strong as the stranger set his arm about her shoulders, assisting her into his home. In another world she may have appraised his warm, strong touch, but for now she was merely grateful for the help. "By the way, I'm Libby."

"Nice to meet you. I'm Heath."

Inside, it took her eyes a moment to adjust to the dimness.

"Sorry about the mess." After leading her to a dilapidated yet comfy brown plaid sofa, he plucked a couple dirty shirts from the back of a wood rocker and a ladder-back kitchen chair. "It's just me around here, and, well…" He shoved his hands in his pockets. "There's not much need to clean."

She waved off his concern. "Considering I've spent the past two years in a tent, the fact that you have an actual roof ranks this place right up there with the Taj Mahal."

"A tent, huh?" He'd ducked in the fridge and emerged with milk, cheese and a carton of eggs. "Sounds like a good story." He set his finds on the butcher-block counter lining the cabin's front wall, then took an energy bar from a cabinet and tossed it to her. "Eat this, then tell me more about how a woman willingly spends two years sleeping under the stars."

Three bites later she'd devoured her snack and drank half the bottled water he'd also given her. "Thank you. That was delicious." She finished off the water, then patted her hands to her bulging belly. "Long story short, the father of this little gal considered himself a free spirit. He believed houses were the equivalent of cells, and marriage a life sentence."

Beating eggs, her savior asked, "You're talking about this guy in the past tense. Is he…dead?"

"Gosh, no." Though too many times than she'd liked, she could've cheerfully clubbed him. "Liam left me for a woman who makes fresh flower headbands. We all traveled together in an unofficial craft show circuit. I'm a potter."

"No kidding?" She didn't miss his raised eyebrows when he shot her a glance. Used to be, that kind of look by so-called acceptable society sent her dashing off for a discreet cry, but no more. She was done apologizing for the life she loved. "You make bowls and vases and stuff?"

"Uh huh."

"Eat up." He handed her a plate filled with eggs scrambled with cheese and two slices of whole wheat toast with butter.

"Oh, wow. This looks delicious. Thanks."

"No problem." After handing her another bottled water, he spun a kitchen chair around and straddled it, resting his forearms on the back. "Should've asked sooner, but want me to call anyone for you? There's gotta be someone you know who'd want to help."

She shook her head. "It's complicated."

"Yeah, well…" He looked to the door. "Make yourself at home, and I'll see what I can do with your car."

"I should probably tag along." She reached beside her for the oversize hobo bag serving as her purse.

"Don't sweat it. I've got this."

"You sure?"

"Yeah. But I'll need your keys." His half grin did funny things to her insides—or maybe it was just the satisfaction of for once having a full stomach. Regardless, she took her first in-depth look at her new friend and was duly impressed. Dark, slightly overgrown buzz cut and the most amazing pale green eyes. He wore desert camo fatigues, boots and a sand-colored T-shirt that hugged his pecs in a way a woman in her condition shouldn't notice.

Distracting herself from the unexpectedly hot view, she fished for her keys and handed them over.

"Thanks," he said. "Be back soon, okay?"

She nodded, and then just as abruptly as he'd entered her life, he was gone.

Hugging her tummy, she said, "Baby, if your daddy was as nice as our new friend, we might not be in such a pickle."

Tilting her head back, Libby groaned.

Despite this temporary respite, she could hardly bear thinking of the hours, let alone days and weeks, to come. She'd thought the journey home would be relatively simple, but it was proving tougher than she'd ever imagined.

"SAM!" DURING THE short return trek to Libby's car, Heath squashed his many questions about the woman by continuing his search for his dog. "You out there, boy?"

The fog had burned off, making for an annoyingly hot and sunny day. No doubt everyone else in town was thrilled, but sun reminded him of days spent on the beach with Patricia and all of the perfect days they'd spent planning out the rest of their perfect lives.

On the main road, again looking to the shoulders for Sam, Heath's stomach knotted in disgust for the guy who'd left Libby on her own while carrying his child. Who did that? Here he'd have selfishly given anything for Patricia to have been with him long enough for them to have a kid, so he'd at least have something tangible beyond pictures to remember her by, yet that lucky asshole was about to have a son or daughter and didn't even care.

Within minutes he made it to Libby's Bug.

He veered his truck around to try giving her vehicle a jump, but the engine wouldn't turn over. The car was an older model he'd only seen while on missions with his navy SEAL unit in developing countries, meaning it didn't even have a gas gauge. Back under the hood he checked the fuel level the way he'd check the oil on any normal car. The stick read nearly a quarter-tank. Which meant he'd reached the end of his personal bag of tricks.

Good thing his cell got better reception on the side of the road than at his cabin.

Thirty minutes later, Hal Kramer arrived with his tow truck.

"Haven't seen one of these in a while," he said, backing out the driver's side door to climb down from his truck. He sauntered over to where Heath stood, wiping sweat from his forehead with a red shop rag. While appraising the situation, he twirled the left side of his handlebar mustache. "Girl I used to date up in Portland drove one of these. Whenever she drank too much wine, I drove. My legs were so long I usually ended up turning off the engine switch with my knee."

"Good times…" Heath said with a faint smile.

The burly town mechanic walked to the vehicle's rear, then lifted the engine cover. "You happen to check the gas and battery?"

"Yep." Hands in his pockets, Heath tried not to remember how frightened he'd been when Libby collapsed at his feet. He'd done his best to hide his fear from her, but inside, he'd been a wreck. Sam's disappearing act already had Heath on edge. The reminder of how frail Patricia had been at the end finished the job of making a normally unflappable guy a nervous wreck.

"All right, old girl." Hal crouched in front of the engine. "Let's take a peek under your knickers…."

While his longtime friend tinkered at the rear of the car, Heath looked inside. A pottery wheel occupied the passenger seat and an assortment of suitcases and boxes had been crammed into the back. When Libby told him she was a potter, he'd honestly thought she'd been joking, but maybe not. Did that mean she'd also been telling the truth about spending two years in a tent?

Oddly enough, if he counted the total time he'd spent on missions, he'd probably slept under the stars more than her, but that was different. Given a choice between a bed and dirt, the bed would always win.

"Try starting it!" Hal called.

Heath gave the engine another try. "Nothing!"

A few curses later, Hal appeared, wiping his hands on his rag. "Thought there might be a quick fix—loose hose or something—but I'm guessing this is electrical. Let me run it into my shop and I'll see what I can find."

"Sounds good." Heath would take Libby to town, where she'd be someone else's problem—not that he'd minded helping, just that with her gone, he could focus on finding his dog. "Have any idea how long it'll take?"

Hal shrugged. "Ten minutes. Ten days. If I need parts, depends on where they are and if the owner has the Ben Franklins to buy 'em."

Heath released a long, slow exhale. "Yeah... What if the owner's short on cash?"

"Is he from around here?"

"Nah. Belongs to a woman—she's passing through. The reason I ask is she's very pregnant, broke and must weigh less than a soaked kitten."

Scratching his head, Hal said, "Sorry to hear it. I'll certainly do what I can to keep costs down, but with vintage models like this I can't make any promises."

"I understand. I'll bring her round a little later. You two can sort out an arrangement."

"Sounds good."

Heath shook his old friend's hand, then helped him load Libby's car. With any luck the repair would be fast and cheap, getting her back on the road to wherever she'd been going.

And if the fix wasn't fast and proved expensive?

He closed his eyes, pinching the bridge of his nose. He hated being an ass, but if Libby had to stick around, he'd just have to make sure she stayed away from him.

Chapter Two

Libby woke from a nap to the sound of someone splitting logs with an ax. Having spent many nights warmed by a campfire, she'd grown familiar with the rhythmic thwack and thump.

She'd curled into a ball on the sofa. A glance down showed she'd thoughtfully been covered by a soft, mossy-green blanket that'd even been tucked around her perpetually cold toes.

Rising and keeping the blanket around her like a shawl, she went in search of her host, assuming he was the one outside chopping.

She found him wearing no shirt and wielding an ax. His chest was broad enough to have earned its own zip code. No way was she even allowing her glance to settle long enough on his honed abs and pecs to give them a formal appraisal. Suffice it to say, he was built better than any man she'd seen outside of a movie.

Considering the cooler air and how low on the horizon the sun had dipped, she called, "Have I been asleep as long as I'm afraid I have?"

He cast a wary glance in her direction. "Yep. You snoozed right through lunch. There's a sandwich for you in the fridge. If you're still hungry, I can heat up some soup."

"I'm sure a sandwich will be fine. Thanks."

"No problem." He brought the ax down hard on his latest log. "After you eat, I'll run you into town. You were out cold when I got back from looking at your car, but I couldn't fix the problem. It ended up having to be towed."

"Oh." Stomach knotted with dread over what the repair may cost, she forced her breathing to slow. As much as she hated the thought, was now the time to officially cry uncle by asking for help? *No.* When she met with her parents, it'd be on her own terms. She'd gotten herself into this mess, and she'd get herself out of it. If her father had believed her a dismal failure before, he was in for quite a shock to see her life had only grown that much more pathetic.

"The town mechanic—Hal—does great work. He's honest and does whatever it takes to keep costs low."

"Good. I can't thank you enough for…everything." If he hadn't come along when he did, there's no telling what may have happened. As tightly as she clung to the stubborn streak and refusing to admit further failure to her parents, she'd finally reached the point where if it came down to protecting her baby's health, she'd have no other choice. A sobering fact she preferred dealing with later.

"Go ahead and eat your sandwich." He reached for another log. "I'll be done in a few."

"O-okay…" Was he dismissing her? Though his words were polite, she couldn't escape the feeling that his failure to make small talk or eye contact signaled he'd rather she be on her way.

Not surprising. If she were fortunate enough for this to be her home, she supposed she wouldn't want a stranger hanging around.

Running her fingertips along the rough-hewn porch

rail, she—more than anything—couldn't wait to one day experience what it would feel like to truly belong. To have found her own special niche in the world where she was accepted and appreciated for who she was.

When she'd bolted from the home she'd been raised in, her grand plan had been becoming part of an artistic community, but dreams have a funny way of dissolving when exposed to reality's ugly light.

"Go ahead and start eating," her host nudged. "Last thing I need is for you to suffer another fainting spell."

She cast him a slight smile. "Sure. Sorry. I tend to daydream."

His only response was a nod before reaching for his next log. His actions were needlessly, almost recklessly fast, as if driven by an invisible demon. Though curiosity burned to know more—anything—about this kind man who'd done more for her in an afternoon than anyone else in recent memory, Libby held tight to her questions instead, turning her back on him to enter the cabin.

With any luck she'd soon be on her way and this day and all of the rocky ones before it would fade into a mental collage featuring only happy times and none of the bad.

An hour later, Libby found herself once again alongside Heath in his truck, heading down the main street of the sleepy town of Bent Road. The rich smell of vintage leather seats mixed with his own masculine flavor of wood and sweat. During the whole trip he didn't say a word, other than a brief inquiry as to whether or not she was cold. At first she'd found the silence awkward, but then it brought her an unexpected peace.

With Liam, she'd felt pressured to always be talking. His constant need to be entertained had been exhausting.

The town sat in the midst of dense forest—a sun-dazzled glade forgotten by time. Historic, redbrick buildings held an assortment of businesses from drug and hardware stores to a lawyer's office and dentist. Window boxes and clay pots celebrated summer with eye-popping color. Purple lobelia and red geraniums. Yellow and orange marigolds, mixed with pink and white petunias.

The floral kaleidoscope spoke to her on a long-forgotten level. Along with her dreams of simply having a home, she'd always wished for a garden. Not only would she grow flowers, but tomatoes and green beans and lettuce.

Thick ferns hung from every lamppost, and the sidewalks were made of weathered brick.

With the truck's windows down, she closed her eyes and breathed deeply. The briny Pacific blended with the sweet flowers, creating a heady fragrance she wouldn't soon forget.

Around the next bend stood an old-style strip-and-cabin motel. A sign built in the shape of a smiling, gingham-clad couple with rosy cheeks proclaimed in red neon that the place was named the Yodel Hoo Inn. Swiss chalet-styled, the dark log structure's every paned window were framed by sunny, yellow shutters. The paint was cracked and a little faded, but that didn't stop it from being fun. Towering pines embraced it and the attached diner. Thriving hanging flower baskets added still more pops of color.

"Everything's so pretty," Libby said more to herself than Heath.

He grunted. "Fourth of July fishing tourney, art festival and carnival's only a little over a week away. Whole damn town goes overboard with decorating. Lucky for you, you won't be around when the eight-hundred miles of red, white and blue bunting rolls out."

"Sounds amazing."

"Sure—as long as you don't get roped into helping take it all down."

He slowed the truck then turned into a gas station that had two pumps and a four-stall garage, each humming with activity. Her Bug sat midway up a hydraulic lift. The engine cover was open and three men stood around it in animated discussion, staring and pointing.

"That can't be good," she noted while Heath parked next to a tow truck with Hal's Garage emblazoned across the door.

"What?"

"All those guys debating over my car. In my perfect fantasy world, I'd hoped it was already fixed, and the mechanic wouldn't have minded trading his services for one of my best clay pots."

"Uh, yeah. I don't think Hal does pots." Eyes narrowed, his befuddled look was one to which she'd sadly grown accustomed to seeing in others. Instead of viewing a glass as half-full, she saw it as bubbling over with a splash of orange and a maraschino cherry. Liam had constantly harped at her to be more realistic, but why? What did it hurt to be happy? Or at least, try?

After turning off the engine, Heath looked to her bulging belly, then asked, "Need help getting out?"

"No, thanks." She cast him a smile. "I think I've got it."

But then she creaked open her door, only to get her purse hooked around the seat belt, which left her hanging at a steep angle.

As was starting to be the norm, her rescuer anticipated her needs and was there to help before she could even ask.

"Sure you're ready for motherhood?" he teased, untangling her purse strap.

"Ha-ha..." She should probably be offended by his question, but little did he know, she'd wondered the same since learning she carried Liam's baby.

"How about trying this again, only with me here to catch you." He grazed his hand to her outer thigh, helping her swing her legs around. His touch proved electric, which was surprising, given her condition. Then he took her hands, guiding her the rest of the way down. Even though she'd set her sandal-clad feet to solid ground, her legs felt shaky beneath her. She needn't have worried, though, as Heath stepped in again, cupping his hand around her elbow to help keep her steady.

"Thanks." She tried acting normal, even though her runaway pulse was anything but!

"No problem." Easing his arm around her waist, he asked, "Wanna just wait in the truck, and I'll give you a report on what Hal found?"

"That's sweet of you to offer, but you've already done enough. I wish I had some way to repay you."

He waved off her gratitude. "Anyone in my position would do the same."

No, they wouldn't. Her ex was proof.

"Those guys standing around your car?"

"Yes?" She waddled around the garage's south side.

"The big one with the 'stache is Hal. The other two are his twin sons—Darryl and Terryl. They're identical, save for one's a crazy Dodgers fan, and the other's crazy about the Mariners. You may want to avoid them when the two teams play—not a good time."

She laughed. "I appreciate the advice. Hopefully, your friend Hal will get me back on my way in the next hour or so."

Famous last words.

After introductions—Libby hid her smile upon noticing the twins wearing hats from their respective baseball teams—Hal shook his head and frowned.

"Wish I had better news for you." He tucked a shop rag in his shirt pocket. "Electrical system's shot. Fried like Sunday-supper chicken."

Libby's stomach knotted so hard it startled the baby. She rubbed the tender spot where she'd kicked. "But you can fix it, right?"

"Well, sure. Me and my boys can fix damn near anything—pardon my French."

"You're pardoned. Just please tell me you've got the parts and I'll be on my way before sunset."

Darryl laughed. Or, it might've been Terryl. She'd forgotten which team each preferred.

The one wearing a Dodgers cap said, "Ma'am, finding all these parts is gonna take me hours—maybe days— on the internet. You'll be lucky if you're out of here in a month."

"You hush." Hal elbowed his son. Turning to Libby, he said, "You have my solemn word that I'll get your ride fixed as soon as possible. But I'm afraid my boy's right—it ain't gonna be fast, easy or cheap."

"Oh?" Stress knotted her throat. Was this really happening? She barely had enough cash for the gas she'd need for the rest of her drive to Seattle. There was no way she'd have enough for repairs and staying over however long it took to get the work done.

Swallow your pride and ask Mom and Dad for help.

Libby raised her chin. No way would she surrender just yet. "You don't really think it'll take a month to find parts, do you?"

Hal shrugged. "No telling till we get started."

Hugging herself, she nodded.

Heath didn't do tears, so when he noted Libby's eyes filling, he slipped back into take-charge mode. "Hal, do what you can, and since Libby doesn't have a cell, keep me posted."

"Will do."

To Libby, Heath said, "Let's see what we can do about finding you a cheap place to stay."

"I—I'll figure it out," she assured him. "I'm grateful for all you've done, but I can take it from here."

"Motel's just down the road a piece." Hal barked at his sons to quit lollygagging and get back to work. "Tell Gretta I sent you and she'll discount your rate."

"I think I have more pull with her than you," Heath said, already guiding Libby back to his truck.

"Wouldn't be so sure about that. She told me you missed Sunday supper yet again."

Heath ignored Hal's comment. He had his reasons for missing most every Stone gathering, and his mother damn well knew it.

It took all of three minutes to reach the inn that had been in his family since the 1940s, when Bent Road had been a weekend fishing mecca for Portland, Seattle and even San Francisco's wealthy vacationers. In the 1930s, the CCC or Civilian Conservation Corp, had provided badly needed infrastructure to the area to allow for its growth. But when a 1942 wildfire destroyed the row of vacation homes that had lined the coastal bluffs, the town's soul suffered a direct blow. The motel was lucky to have survived the fire.

Decades later, Bent Road's tourism consisted of Heath's family's place, and a few fishing lodges specializing in charter trips on the Umpqua River.

"This Gretta we're meeting is your mom?"

"Yeah." Heath had been so lost in thought, he'd momentarily forgotten Libby was with him.

"Do you two not get along?"

"We're good. It's complicated."

Her laugh struck him as sad. "I can relate."

When he pulled onto the inn's blacktop drive, she gasped. "This adorable place belongs to you?"

"Not me, but my mom. My dad died a long time ago."

"I'm sorry."

He shrugged, then parked the truck and killed the engine.

"Sit tight till I get around to help you climb out. We don't need you getting tangled again."

Heath hated the heaviness in his chest at Libby's continued intrusion upon his life, but he hadn't been raised to turn away someone in need. His time in the navy had only reinforced that tradition. Still, he needed to get back to his cabin. Resume his search for Sam, then get back to his new normal—a life he wasn't proud of, but at the moment, it was the best he had to give.

After helping Libby safely to her feet, he hovered alongside her, unable to shake the feeling of her being precious cargo. His mom never turned away a stray, and hopefully, she'd view Libby in the same light.

Just then his mom rounded the corner of the front office with her watering can in hand. "Hey, stranger." Gretta believed customers appreciated employees wear-

ing gingham getups that matched the inn's sign, so in
addition to her salt-and-pepper hair being braided, she
wore a checkered red dress with matching red sneakers.

Her hug made him feel like the world's worst son for
not having been by to see her sooner.

"Hi, I'm Gretta Stone." She extended her free hand to
Libby. "Looks like you swallowed a watermelon seed."

Heath died a little inside. *Really, Mom?*

Fortunately, Libby laughed. "Yes, ma'am, I did. Hope
the baby doesn't come out red-and-green." Her smile was
accompanied by a wink. Meeting his mom's outstretched
hand, she said, "I'm Libby Dewitt. Nice to meet you."

"Likewise." To her son, she asked, "To what do I owe
this pleasure? I know you didn't stop by just to see me."

He'd wondered how long it would take her to get a
dig in about his lack of recent visits. "Actually, I was
out looking for Sam this morning and stumbled across
Libby instead. Her car broke down, and—"

"Wait." His mom held up her hand, stopping him mid-
sentence. "Libby, I want to hear all about your poor car,
but Sam is my son's dog. Sounds like we need to launch
a search party."

"For sure," Libby said. She turned to Heath. "Why
didn't you say something when I first got here? Your dog
is way more important than my busted ride."

Uncomfortable with having his problems on public
display, Heath rammed his hands in his pockets. "I'll
find him."

"Of course you will. With my help. And Libby, would
I be right in assuming you're needing a temporary place
to stay?"

"Yes, ma'am."

"Great." Gretta watered the plant nearest her. "Let me get you set up in a room, then—"

"Sorry for interrupting," Libby said, "but I'm strapped for cash. Think we could work out some sort of trade for a room?"

"What'd you have in mind?"

Never had Heath wished more to be a dishonorable man. All he wanted to do was get back to his cabin and resume his search for Sam—alone. He didn't want his well-meaning mom involved, and he sure didn't need the added concern of worrying whether or not Libby was on the verge of going into labor.

"I might not look like it," Libby said, "but I'm a hard worker. I could waitress at the diner. Clean rooms for you or do laundry. Run your front desk—pretty much any odd job you need done. I'm a potter by trade, so I can also make any sort of custom piece you might like."

Was it wrong of Heath that this was one time he wished his mom would turn away a stray? He had nothing against Libby. She seemed like a great gal. That didn't change the fact that in her condition, she needed to find a home base—fast. And Bent Road wasn't it.

Come on, Mom. Just say no.

Gretta once again extended her hand for Libby to shake. "You have a deal. I just happen to have a vacancy, as well as a family reunion fishing group who are really going through the towels. I've had the washer and dryer going practically 24/7, and could sure use help."

Libby's shoulders sagged. Relieved? "Thank you, ma'am. I promise I won't be any trouble, and just as soon as my car's ready, I'll be on my way."

Heath tried not to scowl. Libby was now officially his

mother's concern, so why didn't he feel better? Maybe because her pretty, misty-eyed smile tugged at his long-frozen heart?

Chapter Three

Libby sat on the foot of her new bed—the first true bed she'd slept on in two years, and could hardly believe her good fortune. Her constantly aching back practically sang! Beneath his curmudgeonly exterior, Heath was a sweetheart. After meeting his mom, Libby knew why.

Her new boss had given her fifteen minutes to "freshen up," then asked her to man the inn's front office desk while she traipsed around the woods for her son's dog. They'd both agreed night hiking probably wasn't a good idea for a woman in Libby's condition.

After splashing cold water on her face and running a brush through her hair, Libby still couldn't get over the wonder of her situation. She'd grown to appreciate the unique flavor of her rustic life, but a part of her had always wished Liam wanted more. Not just for them to share an apartment or house, but a commitment. She'd assumed he'd one day see the light—her light, their shared light—but she couldn't have been more wrong.

Hugging the baby, she said, "I'm sorry in advance for the mess you'll be born into. Once our car's fixed, there's no telling how my folks are going to take the news about you. In a perfect world, they'll love you like I already do, but…"

She shut up in favor of grabbing a tissue to blot her teary eyes and blow her suddenly runny nose. What happened to her usually sunny disposition?

Instead of looking for possible trouble somewhere down the road, she needed to count her current blessings. Starting by meeting Gretta in the inn's cozy lobby.

The early evening had turned crisp and she found the conifer-laced air invigorating.

Up close, the inn was even more charming than she'd seen from the road. Steam rose from a small pool in a glade near the office, around which sat a group of six guys, laughing over beers. A gazebo, wreathed in ivy, ferns and thriving impatiens graced the grounds' far end. A glider swing and hammock stood amongst still more gardens that faced the row of rooms and a few cabins. Hydrangeas dazzled in shades of blue ranging between cobalt and sky.

The only thing missing from the idyllic scene was Heath's truck. A fact which she shouldn't have even noticed, let alone found the tiniest bit disappointing. He'd already done more than most anyone else would've given the circumstances. So why did she still want more? Oh, she didn't want things from him like food or transportation, but rather she had a sudden craving for his company.

"There you are." Gretta stepped out of the office. "I was just coming to find you."

"Here I am," Libby said with a nervous laugh, still not quite believing her luck over having stepped into such a perfect situation. "Reporting for duty."

"Good, good…" She held open the plate glass door, ushering Libby inside. "Is your room okay? Find everything you need?"

"It's beautiful—and so homey. The gingham curtains

and vintage logging pics make it feel like a place you'd want to stay a nice long while."

Heath's mom beamed. "I'm so glad you like it. My son thought I was off my rocker for spending so much on redecorating last year, but my business has more than doubled, so he can keep any further advice to himself."

Laughing, Libby said, "Hands-down, the room you've loaned me is way more inviting than his cabin—not that I wasn't thankful he found me, but—" Libby felt horrible that her statement made it sound as though she was dissing the man who'd done so much "I'm sorry, that came out wrong. Heath's cabin is perfect. I just meant that you'd win should the two of you be in a decorating contest."

"I get it," Gretta said with another warm smile. "And I thank you. Though, in Heath's defense, home decor was never really his cup of tea. Now, his wife, Patricia, on the other hand…" A cloud passed over Gretta's once sunny expression. "Well, she was a pro."

"Was?" Libby asked.

"Poor girl died of cancer. For a while there we all thought Heath might go with her. It's been nearly fourteen months, but nobody seems able to reach him."

"I—I'm sorry." What Libby went through in having Liam leave her was bad enough; she couldn't even imagine the pain of losing a spouse.

Gretta shrugged. "By the time you get to be my age, you realize death's an inevitable side effect of life. But it's never easy seeing a young person go. Feels unnatural."

Not sure what else to do or say, Libby nodded.

"Anyway…" Gretta took a deep breath, only to let the air rush out. "Since my rooms are all full, you shouldn't have to do a thing, other than grab a few towels or ring up snacks, but I always like someone to be up here—just in case. If you run into any trouble, here's my cell." She jotted the number on a Post-it, then stuck it on a computer screen. She did a quick run-through on the register, then showed Libby what was available in terms of food and sundries in the lobby's small gift section. "Think you can manage?"

"Easy peasy," Libby said, despite this being her first real job in a while, outside of selling her art.

"Good." Heath's mom took her purse from beneath the front desk and headed for the door. "Oh—and thanks again for filling in. I'm not sure my son could handle losing his wife and his dog."

HEATH CUPPED HIS HANDS to his mouth. "Sam! Come on, boy!"

Where the hell could he be?

The deeper Heath trudged into the forest, the madder he got—not just at his mutt, who knew better than to run off, but at the world in general.

As relieved as he'd been to escape Libby's perma-smile and adorably huge belly, he was also resentful of the man who'd turned his back on her. Since losing his wife, Heath had no tolerance for men who willingly shirked their responsibilities in regard to their women. He hadn't noticed a ring on Libby's left hand, which led him to assume the baby's father hadn't even married her to give his future child a name. Who did that?

"Sam!" he bellowed. "Get your ass home!"

A good half mile off, car headlights shone in the direction of Heath's cabin.

His mom, arriving to save the day?

He loved her. He honestly didn't mean for them to always be at odds, but for as long as he could remember, she'd had the need to save every broken animal and person in her world. What she couldn't seem to grasp was the fact that he was beyond saving. He had, for all practical purposes, died with Patricia—even his CO had said as much when he'd sent him packing. Being put on indefinite leave for failure to perform his duties had been one of Heath's greatest shames, but what was done was done.

No going back now.

"Heath?" His mom's voice carried through the ever-darkening gloom. "Where are you, hon?"

He groaned. Why couldn't she just go away?

If, God forbid, the worst had happened to Sam, the last thing Heath wanted was an audience when he broke down.

"Heath?" She sounded closer—a lot closer, when she rounded the trail's nearest bend. "There you are."

"God, Mom, I told you I've got this handled."

She shined a high-beam flashlight in his eyes. "Have you found him yet?"

"No."

"Then you obviously haven't handled squat."

"You look like you're about to pop," said one of the inn's fishermen to Libby after placing a bag of pretzels and a Snickers bar on the chest-high counter. The guy's thick, red curls stuck out the bottom of a hat covered in fishing lures. "When're you due?"

"Third week in July." Libby knew she should have looked forward to her child's entry into the world, but with her life so uncertain, the only thing the date brought was dread.

He whistled. "My wife just had our fifth, and I thought

you look awfully close to the big day. Know what you're having?"

"A girl." Libby forced her usual smile. "I'm excited to finally meet her, but also a little scared."

"You'll be fine," the kindly man said with a wink. "Although, my wife would smack me if I went so far as calling labor easy."

Laughing, Libby said, "Honestly? That's the least of my worries. It's what happens once I take my baby home that has me spooked."

Even thirty minutes after the man left, Libby couldn't resume her interest in the romantic comedy she'd borrowed from Gretta's extensive library.

Libby's perch on the desk stool unfortunately afforded an excellent view of the landline phone.

It stared at her, taunted her, made her feel like a fool for not having long since dialed her parents' familiar number.

She'd always heard about the evils of pride, but lately, she felt at constant war with the emotion. Was it pride keeping her from crawling back to her folks in her current defeated state? Or self-preservation? With a baby on the way, did she even have the right to put her own desires ahead of her child's basic needs and protection?

Pressing the heels of her hands to her forehead, she willed an answer to come, when clearly this wasn't a simple black-and-white decision, but one shaded with a myriad of grays.

At her high school graduation dinner, when her parents told her that to pursue a career in art was ridiculous, that after college she was destined to spend a few years in a low-profile advertising position, then settle into a life

as a society wife and mom—just like her own mother—
Libby had initially rebelled by running with a bad crowd.

That summer, a protest rally gone horribly wrong had
landed her in jail for vandalism. Her father had bailed her
out, but basically handed her the edict that from here on
out, it was either his way or she needed to hit the highway. She'd chosen the highway, and with him calling
her a disappointment and loser on her way out his front
door, she'd never looked back.

In the five years since leaving her prestigious Seattle address, she'd spoken only to her mother, and only
on Christmas. Each time, her mother had begged her to
come home. When Libby asked if her father's opinion of
her lifestyle had changed, and her mother reported it had
not, Libby politely ended their conversations and prayed
that by the next year, her father would come around.

The fact that she was now broke, knocked up by a
man who'd left her and she didn't even own a running
car proved that everything her father had said about her
being a loser was true. Was she destined to become a
bad mom, as well?

"I DON'T FEEL comfortable leaving you."

"Go. I'm fine." Heath crossed his arms in a defensive
posture. For the past two hours, he and his mom had
crisscrossed the family land, looking for his dog. When
they had no luck, she'd turned chatty, which only pushed
him deeper inside his own tortured thoughts. Was Sam
dead? Lying hurt somewhere?

Images of the dog led Heath's mind's eye to Patricia's
dark last days. She'd been in such pain and he'd been
powerless to do anything to help, other than demand
more meds. To feel such helplessness for a woman he'd

loved so insanely, deeply, completely had been far worse on him than any physical pain he might one day endure.

Having loved the deepest, and now hurt the deepest, what else was left?

"Great," his mom said. "You're *fine*—again. Only, clearly you're not, so whether you like it or not, I'll get Uncle Morris to look after the motel tomorrow, then I'll be out to help search for Sam."

"For the last time…" Heath cocked his head back, staring up at the stars. Common sense told him he needed all the help he could get in looking for Sam, but a sick foreboding got in the way. If the worst had happened, Heath would somehow have to deal with it in his own private way. "Thanks, but no thanks. I just want to be left alone."

"Duly noted." She took her keys from her jeans front pocket, then kissed his cheek. "See you first thing in the morning."

"RUN INTO ANY TROUBLE?" Gretta asked Libby the next morning from behind the wheel of her forest-green Ford Explorer. The fog had been as thick as it was the day before, but by nine, warm sun had rapidly burned it off.

"Nope. Everything was quiet, just like you'd expected." It'd been late when Gretta returned from Heath's, so they hadn't had much time to talk. It had been a long day, and Libby had struggled to keep her eyes open.

In her cozy room, she'd changed into pajamas and reveled in the luxury of indoor plumbing. When she'd slipped between cool sheets and eased her head onto not one, but two downy pillows, for the first time in months, she'd happily sighed with contentment.

Cupping her hands to her belly, she'd closed her eyes

and smiled. But then her eyes popped open. All she could think of while drifting off to sleep was Heath.

The kind of warmhearted, honorable man she'd always secretly yearned for, but knew a broken mess like her would never deserve.

"Thanks for riding out here with me." Gretta turned onto the desolate road leading to Heath's dirt lane. "I'll have to introduce you to my brother when we get back. Morris has been married four—maybe five times?" She scratched her head. "After three I lost count. He's a hopeless romantic. He retired from the navy, made a fortune in the private sector and now I swear his only goal in life is making me crazy, asking for love advice." She paused for air. "He is a doll about helping out with the motel, though. He loves to cook, so the diner's his baby. The motel and restaurant have been in our family for generations. The two of us grew up in the little house behind it. After Heath's dad died, I moved back."

"It's good you and Morris are close." Libby angled on the seat as best she could to face Heath's mom. "I'm an only child, but always wanted a brother or sister."

Gretta snorted. "Be careful what you wish for. Having a sibling hasn't been all sunshine and roses. Morris and my husband—God rest his soul—used to get into horrible rows."

"Oh?" Libby didn't bother asking why, since she assumed chatty Gretta would soon enough fill her in with the details.

"My Vinnie—Heath's father—was a no-nonsense man. I guess twenty years in the military will do that to a person. Not long after he took retirement, we moved back here to take over the motel from my parents. Heath was such a moody teen in those days. He's named after

Heathcliff from *Wuthering Heights*. Never did I think he'd turn out to have the character's same brooding disposition. Did I curse my own son?"

"I'm sure not." Although Libby had been curious about Vinnie and Morris's feud, anything about the elusive Heath was infinitely more entertaining. "Has he always been quiet and gloomy?"

"Not at all. In high school he was homecoming king, and made quite a splash on the basketball team. Everyone loved him—but he had his occasional spells when he enjoyed going off in the woods for fishing and hunting. In the navy—did you know he was a SEAL? He was all the time earning medals. But when he lost Patricia, he just gave up. Breaks my heart. Really does."

"I'm sure."

"Another thing that gets my goat is…"

Libby politely acknowledged Gretta's latest monologue, regarding her neighbor's refusal to plant an appropriate amount of potted flowers for the upcoming Independence Day festivities. But mostly, she stared out at the wall of green on either side of the road, wondering at the vast, remote stretch of land and the odds of Heath ever finding his dog.

Funny, a day earlier, though Libby always viewed her cup as half-full, lately, she'd begun doubting this practice. Beyond her healthy pregnancy, pretty much nothing before meeting the Stones had gone right. Now that she'd heard even part of Heath's tragic story, she was embarrassed for believing she had problems at all. No one had died—well, unless she counted the small piece of herself she'd have to abandon upon returning to her parents' home. She didn't doubt for a moment they'd take her and her baby in, but with the expectation she play by their rules, tossing aside her own hopes and dreams.

AFTER A FITFUL night's sleep, Heath woke at dawn to resume his search for Sam.

He'd been out a few hours, then returned to the cabin to grab energy bars and more water.

The previous night, when his mom told him she'd be back, he'd hoped Uncle Morris was so busy with the diner that he wouldn't be able to help with the motel—in fact, he'd have rather she sent her brother as her proxy. Heath's easygoing uncle wasn't constantly nagging with questions, and he sure as hell would never be so insensitive as to suggest he "climb back on his horse" to find a new love as Gretta occasionally liked to do.

What kind of Happy Land planet was his mom living on that she believed for one second he'd ever be able to replace Patricia? The very idea was insulting.

After downing a piece of white bread smeared with peanut butter, he was loading bottled water into his knapsack when a car roared down his road.

While his initial thought was to punch a hole through the nearest wall, he soon enough realized that since his home was built of logs, that might not be such a great idea for his fist.

A minute later he glanced out the open front door to see his mom's perpetual smile. Making matters worse was the fact that she'd dragged Libby along with her.

Hands in his pockets, he did the right thing by heading out to the SUV to greet them, though he wanted nothing to do with either of their cheery smiles.

"Any luck?" his mom asked, first out of the car.

"Nope."

Libby had opened her door, but clearly needed help getting out. On autopilot, he went to her, steeling himself to ignore her pretty floral smell and the way her petite frame made him feel oversized and all thumbs. "Here we go again...."

"This does feel familiar." Her friendly grin did uncomfortable things to his gut. Made him wistful for days when he used to have an easy smile. Now nothing was easy—especially being around this very pregnant woman who reminded him all too much of what he'd always dreamed his life would be.

"Libby," his mom said, "I didn't even think to ask, but did you have breakfast?"

"No, ma'am."

Gretta conked her forehead. "I'm the worst hostess ever." She turned toward the cabin. "Let me whip up grub for us all, then we'll start our search. Heath, how about showing Libby the bench Grandpa made for your grandmother."

Lips pressed tight, Heath looked to the sky, willing patience for his mom to rain down on him.

"She's a pistol," Libby noted.

"That's one way of putting it." He gestured toward the pine needle–strewn trail leading to the property's bluff. "Feel up to a short walk?"

"Sure, though I'm not exactly steady."

"Let me take your arm—just in case. Last thing I need on top of my missing dog is a busted-up pregnant lady."

Laughing, she shook her head. "Thanks. I think?"

He shot her a sideways glance and came damn close to cracking his own grin while taking hold of her arm. It couldn't have been over fifty yards to the bluff, but worry over his guest's well-being had Heath working up a sweat.

Finally, they made it. Heath tried corralling Libby onto the bench his grandfather made as a romantic gift decades earlier, but she wasn't having it.

"Look at this view…." The awe he used to feel for the land rang through in her breathy tone. "It's amazing. The sun looks like diamonds on the water. Don't you feel like you can see all the way to Japan?"

"Don't get too close to the edge." She stood only a foot away from the two-hundred-foot drop.

"I'm fine," she assured him. "I've always had a great sense of—" In turning to face him, she wobbled.

Heath ran to her, tugging her into the safety of his arms. "Why can't you listen?"

With her baby bump pressed against areas it had no business being, he set her a safe distance back while trying to figure out why just touching her produced such visceral results.

"I told you I was fine," she snapped. "Stop being such a worrywart."

Arms folded, he said, "My apologies for yet again charging to your rescue."

She held her arms defensively crossed over her chest, as well. "Did it ever occur to you that I don't need saving? That I'm doing fine all on my own?"

"Which is why you're living on charity until your car gets fixed? Even then, how are you planning to reimburse Hal?" The moment the acidic questions left Heath's mouth, he regretted them. He especially regretted the telltale signs of tears shimmering in Libby's sky-blue eyes. "I'm sorry."

He approached her, held out his hands to maybe touch her, but then thought better and backed away.

"Doesn't matter," she said with a shrug. "What would an apology help when what you said is true?"

"Yeah, but…" She'd returned to the ledge, which made his pulse race uncomfortably. Why the hell couldn't she just behave?

"Stop. I'm sorry your mom dragged me out here. After we eat, I'll ask her to take me back to the motel, and with any luck, you'll never see me again."

"Libby…" He rammed his hands into his pockets. In an odd way, even saying her name felt uncomfortably intimate.

"No, really, just hush. You're not the only one with troubles, you know? Maybe I didn't lose a spouse, but—"

"Mom told you about Patricia?"

Hand over her mouth, she nodded.

Was nothing sacred?

"I'm sorry for your loss, but that doesn't give you the right to take your pain out on others—especially your sweet mom."

No longer in the mood for sightseeing, Heath turned his back on the pint-size pain in his ass by heading back down the trail.

"What?" she called after him. "You got your feelings hurt, so you're just going to leave?"

Had she been a dude, he'd have flipped her a backhanded bird.

"Fine! Be that way!" she hollered after him. "Being sad won't fix anything, you know! Just makes you more sad, and—"

When she punctuated her sentence with a yelp, despite his frustration, he turned and ran in her direction.

What the hell kind of trouble had she gotten herself into this time?

Only once he reached her, he found her yards down the bluff, pointing to a limp ball of fur, far down on the rocks below. Heath's mouth went dry, and his stomach roiled.

"I-is that your dog?"

Chapter Four

Caring little about his own personal safety, Heath sprinted a few hundred more yards down the bluff's edge until he reached the only somewhat sane route to the crashing surf.

After losing Patricia, he'd sworn to never pray again, and he held that promise even now. The concrete hardening his emotions told him this mission was all about recovery rather than rescue. As much as he'd loved that dog, no way would Heath leave Sam's body exposed to be pecked off bit by bit by scavengers.

The ground constantly gave way beneath him, as the rocks clattered in what had become a dangerous slide. Had he the slightest lick of good sense, he would have gone farther down the bluff to the established trail he usually used to access the beach, but in this case, urgency won over practicality.

Upon finally reaching the rocky shore, he ran until his lungs ached.

There was no hurry. No way even a tough guy like Sam could've possibly survived that fall, so why couldn't Heath stop running to get to him? Why couldn't he shake the feeling that just as it had on that sunny day when Patricia had slipped from him, his life was spinning out of control.

Sure, Sam was just a dog, but most days that mutt felt like the only thing keeping Heath sane. Sam gave him a reason to get up every morning. Beyond the necessities of keeping him fed and watered and letting him in and out, Heath had found solace in watching his dog's tail wag the whole ride to their favorite fishing hole, or hearing him bark when the mutt chased after his ratty old tennis ball.

Twenty yards out, Heath hunched over, bracing his hands on his knees. He couldn't bear going farther.

Eyes squeezed shut, all he saw was the hospice nurse dragging that damned yellow sheet over Patricia's dear, faint smile. Ever since, he'd hated the color almost as much as he hated life.

"What're you doing?" a faint, wind-tossed voice called from above. "Hurry, Heath! We need to get him to a vet."

What was wrong with her?

Couldn't she see he was in pain? Why was she even there, when all he wanted was to be left alone?

"Run!" she hollered.

In a mental fog, Heath raised his gaze to Libby, only to find her animated and waving toward poor Sam's lifeless body. What was wrong with her that at a time like this, she refused to give him space?

"Heath, look at him! He's trying to wag his tail! Don't you know he's alive?"

Alive?

She might as well have been speaking Latin for all the sense the word made in Heath's grief-stricken mind. Hope had long since left his vocabulary.

But then a strange thing happened....

Seagulls rioted near Sam's body, and Sam gave a short *woof,* sending the birds flying.

Charging to action, Heath made it to Sam's side in well under a minute. He kneeled to scoop Sam into his arms, and instead of the cold, salt water–matted fur he'd expected, he was met with solid warmth, a whimper, a feeble tail wag.

Was he dreaming? Had he really been given this second chance?

A quick inspection of his dog showed why Sam hadn't come home. His feet were covered in purple sea urchin spikes. The urchins weren't poisonous, but clearly painful and if it hadn't already, infection was likely to set in.

Shooting to action, uncaring of his own comfort, Heath knelt in the rising surf. Cold water soaked his legs, but he ignored any physical pain to gingerly pluck spike after spike from the swollen and clearly tender pads of Sam's paws.

"Hang in there," Heath soothed, 100 percent focused on the task at hand. "We'll get all of these things out, then run you to the vet. In a few days, you'll be good as new."

Once again having purpose drove Heath to work even more efficiently. Guilt for not having thought to look for Sam on the beach much sooner caused acid to rise from his stomach and high into his throat until bile flavored his tongue.

"I'm sorry," Heath said, stroking behind the dog's silky ears.

Sam whined, lurching forward when Heath tugged at a particularly large and deep spike.

"Be gentle," a soft voice said behind him. Libby had somehow waddled her way to the beach and lowered herself onto a sun-bleached driftwood log.

"You shouldn't be down here." Though he couldn't have begun to explain why, Heath resented her presence.

As a man who'd spent years in the business of saving others, it was a rush to once again be on the job. The purpose and drive felt damn good. The knowledge that for once in a very long time he was making a positive difference—if only to his dog—deeply mattered.

"I thought you might need help. What happened? How did he even get down here?"

"How do you think?" he growled. One glance at her crestfallen expression left Heath ashamed of his sharp words. "Sorry. I've got enough on my plate in carrying Sam safely up the bluff. I don't want to have to worry about you, too."

"Who said you had to?"

Having removed all the spikes, Heath wedged his hands under the dog's fragile frame. Due to his negligence in not having remembered how much Sam enjoyed barking at the occasional sea lions who hung out on the point, the dog had been a while without food or water.

Crashing surf must've muted his bark.

"Drop it," Heath said, already heading for the trail.

"Why are you acting like this?" She chased after him, which only made him feel worse, but no way was he slowing. "You should be thrilled Sam's going to be okay."

"I am."

"So would it be too much of a strain to smile?"

"Shouldn't you worry more about keeping your footing on these rocks?" He kept his gaze focused on the winding dirt trail leading up the bluff.

Sam whined.

"Just a few more minutes, boy…" Heath had never wished more he'd kept up with his physical training. Were he in top form, scaling the hill would've been no big deal—not that it was difficult now, he just lacked the speed he'd once had.

"If you'd slow down just a little," Libby yapped, dogging his heels, "I could help soothe him."

"I've got this," he insisted. "*Please*—back the hell off."

She held up her hands, stepping away per his request, but her glistening tears left him feeling dirty inside. What kind of man yelled at a pregnant woman? What had happened to his honor?

Ha! He and honor and giving a damn about anything parted ways around about the same time the love of his life died in his arms.

"Would it kill you to let me in?" The woman might've temporarily let him be, but there she was, right back in his business. "I just want to help you—you know, like you helped me."

"I don't need help." Jaw clenched, Heath kept his gaze focused on the trail, mentally blocking Sam's heartbreaking whimpers.

By the time Heath reached the trailhead at the top of the bluff, the dog's ninety pounds had his untrained muscles screaming. How had he allowed himself to get so out of shape? Was he really so pathetic?

"You found him!" his mother cried as he approached. "Is he all right?"

"Find my keys!" he shouted back.

From behind him, the sounds of Libby's labored breathing did little to improve his mood.

"Would you like me to drive or hold poor Sam on the way to the vet?" Libby asked.

"You have no lap," he managed from between clenched teeth. His thigh muscles screamed from mounting the steep grade. Back when he'd been on the job, a trek like this would've been a cakewalk. Now, when his dog needed him, his body wasn't delivering as it should. And that further pissed him off. But the anger was good. It gave him much-needed energy to fuel the rest of his way to the truck.

"There are very few people I've disliked over the years," she said, "but you, Heath Stone, are definitely one of them. You're thickheaded and stubborn and obstinate."

"Aren't those all basically the same?"

"Well…" His mind's eye pictured her heart-shaped face all flushed and scrunched from concentration. And that image did nothing to improve his already dour mood. Because for the briefest flash of an instant, the thought of her coaxed his smile out of hiding. "They might be the same, but that's okay, because I wanted to emphasize how truly awful you are. When you first rescued me, I thought you were the kindest soul I'd ever encountered, but—"

"Do you ever shut up?"

"No! And for you to suggest it just makes me loathe you that much more."

At the top of the bluff, with both of them breathing heavy, Heath might have found the energy to laugh at her crazy-ass statement if he hadn't been carrying his injured dog. As if he cared if she *loathed* him.

But then, when the trail widened, she passed him, and all those blond curls bounced with her every snappy step. For a woman in her condition, she sure could move. Though from behind, she didn't even look pregnant. In fact, the way the morning sun shone through the flimsy fabric of her dress, not a whole lot of her was left to his imagination. His body's involuntary—and swift—reaction to the sight of her soft curves soured his mood all the more.

"I can't believe he's all right." His mom charged down the trail to meet them. "I set bowls of food and water in the truck."

"Thanks."

She reached to pet Sam, but Heath didn't want to slow his momentum.

"Why're you so prickly?" she asked when he sidestepped her. "Sam's safe. You should be overjoyed."

"I am. But he's not out of the woods yet." *Plus, I just had my first erection caused by a woman other than my wife...*.

"HE'S GOING TO be fine, you know?" While driving Heath's truck, for a split second, Libby took her eyes from the deserted highway to glance toward him and his dog. Sam had long since finished off his water and now started in on his food. His eyes had already brightened, and she found herself liking him much better than his doggy *dad*. "It's okay for you to relax."

"Could you please just focus on the road?"

Gretta followed behind them in her SUV.

Heath sat all stiff and straight and his handsome features were marred by the oddest expression. Was the big, strong guy trying not to cry? She'd been touched by seeing how much Sam meant to Heath. Was there a significance beyond any normal dog bond? Had he shared Sam with his wife?

Though it was none of her business, Libby couldn't help but ask, "Did you and your wife get Sam together?"

For the longest time, Heath remained silent. The way a muscle ticked in his hardened jaw set her on edge.

Had she picked at a wound still too tender for casual conversation?

"I'm sorry." She steered the truck around a small branch that had fallen onto the road. "Please, forget I even asked."

"Yeah…" When he finally did speak, his tone was raspy. He stroked one of Sam's ears. "A friend told us his Lab-collie mix was having a litter, and we picked this guy out as a puppy. He had five littermates, but we could tell right away he was the one. He had spunk. He was always into everything. A little too curious for his own good—which I guess is how he landed in this predicament."

"Poor guy." She patted the dog's head.

A glance at Heath had her thinking he might say something more, but much to her disappointment, he did not. Which made no sense—not so much the lack of conversation, but why his sudden silence bothered her.

THE RELIEF SHIMMERING through him after Sam's positive health report left Heath a little punch-drunk. He'd dodged a bullet with that one. Everyone from his mom and uncle to his old SEAL gang kept telling him it was time to move on. He needed to get on with things. Get back to work. There was always lots of *getting* in their well-meaning speeches, but none of their words amounted to squat when it came to making him feel even a fraction better about having lost his wife.

If he'd then lost her dog, too…

Well, he was just damned lucky it hadn't come to that.

The fact that he ultimately had Libby to thank for spotting Sam didn't escape him. As soon as the dog was doing better, maybe he'd take her to a formal thank-you lunch.

While you're feeling generous, think you owe her an apology for being such an ass on the beach?

Heath folded his arms, focusing on his dog rather than his pansy conscience, which had apparently gone as soft as his out-of-shape body.

"You're one lucky fella," said Cassidy Mitchell, the town veterinarian, while applying the last of Sam's bandages. She'd given him pain meds and antibiotics, and at the moment, with his giant pink tongue lolling and tail lightly thumping the metal exam table, the dog looked about as happy as could be expected. To Heath, the vet said, "Since you live a ways out, I'll send you home with supplies to clean and change these bandages. Once he starts feeling better, he's gonna want to go straight back to his normally wild ways, but just to be safe, I'd keep him inside and resting as much as he'll let you."

"Will do," he said, scooping Sam into his arms.

Gretta had left right after hearing Sam was okay. The commode in room ten had overflowed, and she'd had to meet the plumber. Heath would have called her, but he'd left his cell back at the cabin.

"Think you can handle carrying Sam's supplies?" the vet asked Libby.

Libby nodded, taking the multiple packages Cassidy's assistant had assembled.

"Sure you're okay?" the vet asked Libby. Heath had made brief introductions upon their arrival. "You've paled about ten shades since you first got here."

"I'm fine," Libby said, but having witnessed her previous faint, and seeing her expression look similar now, Heath wasn't so sure.

"Just in case…" The vet's teen assistant trailed them

outside. "Let me take Sam's bandages and meds, and then you just open the truck door."

"You're both being silly." Libby made the trade-off, then opened the door. "I'm abso-lute-lee…"

Fine? Heath finished her sentence just as her legs buckled from beneath her.

Chapter Five

With Sam centered on the truck's bench seat, Heath shot into action, now hefting Libby up next to the dog.

"She okay?" The pimple-faced teen assistant couldn't have been over sixteen. He'd paled as much as Libby.

"Hope so." Heath took Sam's supplies. "I'll run her to the clinic, though, to make sure."

Just as she had during her previous fainting spell, Libby woke within a few seconds. At which point, Heath, for the second time that morning, felt crazy-relieved. And guilty. If she hadn't followed him to the beach to get Sam, would she have passed out?

"Whoa…" She'd rested her head against the seat back, and now pressed her fingertips to her forehead. "What happened?"

"You fainted again."

She groaned. "That's not good."

"Nope. Which is why I'm running you to the doc."

"I'm all right. Please—" she stroked Sam's sleepy face "—take me to my room at the motel. I just need a nap."

"Probably, but I don't want it on my already full plate if it turns out there's something more wrong."

"Look…" Sighing, she hugged her belly. "The truth

is, I can't afford to pay a doctor. I'm good. I *have* to be, because really, I don't have another choice."

"There's always a choice—this time, it's doing the responsible thing for your baby by letting me pay for your treatment."

"That's not necessary. I'm already feeling better."

"Perfect. Then you won't mind me wasting my own money to prove it."

Other than her pressing her lips together a bit tighter, Libby showed no other emotion. He was glad, because the day had been draining enough without her launching another fight.

He pulled to a stop at the red light on Archer.

With the Fourth of July so close, carnies were hard at work assembling rides on the elementary school's soccer field. The Tilt-a-Whirl resembled a praying mantis with its legs still folded on the flatbed trailer where it lived when it wasn't at play.

Back when he'd been a kid visiting his grandparents over the holiday while his dad was on leave, the annual carnival that started on the first was everything. Corn dogs and funnel cakes. Losing a month's allowance worth of quarters on the Coin Dozer game. Best of all, spending time with his family, back when they really had been a family.

The light changed and he made a left, heading toward the clinic.

With Sam peacefully napping and a warm summer breeze riffling his hair through the open windows, Heath could've almost been at peace if it weren't for the faint sniffles of Libby crying.

In no way prepared to deal with drama in the form of female tears—especially the pregnancy tears his married friends warned him were particularly potent—he tightened his grip on the wheel.

A few minutes later, past the fire station and library and the retirement home where, on a trip home for Easter, he and Patricia had teased each other about moving into when they both grew old, Heath pulled into the clinic's freshly blacktopped parking lot. The asphalt sounded sticky beneath the truck's tires and the pungent smell had Libby crinkling her nose.

"This is an all-around bad idea. I feel great. And what're we going to do with Sam?"

Heath drove to the far side of the lot, parking beneath a row of Douglas firs on a section of pavement still old and sun-faded.

Sam was fast asleep, and judging by his snores, would be for a while. The day was fine. The temperature was in the mid-seventies. With the windows down, he'd be equally as content in the truck as he would've been on the living room couch.

"He's gonna nap, just like the vet wanted."

One hand on her belly, the other on her door, Libby still looked unsure. In that instant, she looked so alone and afraid, something in his long-frozen heart gave way.

He wasn't a monster; he was just a man who'd essentially given up on his own life, but that didn't mean he had the right to inflict his messed-up shit on this lost soul.

He tentatively reached out for her, for an endless few seconds, hovering his hand in the neutral zone over Sam before reaching the rest of the way to Libby's forearm. Upon making contact, her vulnerability made him want to be strong. Not for himself, but for this fragile woman with an innocent child growing inside.

After giving her a gentle and what he hoped was a reassuring squeeze, they made eye contact for only an instant. He couldn't have stood more, so he looked away, swallowing hard, wishing his pulse to slow. He was afraid, so very afraid, but of what he couldn't comprehend. "Let's, ah, head inside. Get you checked out."

Her eyes shone, and she also shifted her gaze, sniffling before opening her door.

Heath hustled to her side of the vehicle in order to help her down.

It had been years since he'd been to Doc Meadows, but everyone in town knew appointments were welcome, but if you had something come up, the doctor and his nurse would stay as late as necessary to ensure everyone with a need was seen.

"Sure is pretty for a clinic…." Libby said, peering up at the three-story Victorian.

"Used to belong to one of the summer people."

"Summer people?"

"Rich folks from Portland, even San Francisco, who used to come here to spend their summers on the shore. After the 1942 fire, hardly any homes were left. This one was owned by a bank president whose wife fancied herself to be a *shade tree* architect." Heath was glad for the story. It distracted him from Libby's slow pace—more guilt stemming from the realization that he should have driven her to the door. What kind of idiot was he to have made her walk? "Want me to go get the truck?"

"For what?" She pressed her hands to the small of her back.

"So you don't have to exert yourself."

She waved off his concern. "You worry too much.

And what's up with this new, polite travelogue version of your formerly crotchety self?"

"I'm not crotchety—reserved, maybe. Definitely not crotchety."

"If you say so…" He wasn't sure how she managed, but after casting him an exaggerated wink and grin, she sashayed right past him and mounted the stairs.

"You shouldn't be taking off like that," he urged, staying behind her in case she fell—at least that's the line he fed himself in order to not feel like a creeper for having accidentally caught himself yet again checking out her behind. "Last thing I need is for you to pull another fainting spell."

"I won't," she said from the top of the stairs, even though her exaggerated breathing told him she was winded.

He opened the door for her, ushering her inside the waiting room that his mom told him used to be the front parlor where Ingrid Mortimer—the former lady of the house—served formal tea every summer Sunday afternoon. He was just debating on whether or not to share the information with Libby, when the doctor's receptionist, Eloise Hunter, shot out from behind her desk to usher Libby into a wheelchair.

"You poor thing," Eloise clucked. The woman not only stood six feet tall—not counting her big red hair bun—but she was big around, too. And mean. But then his senior year in high school, she had caught him cutting all the roses from her garden for his latest crush. "Doc Mitchell's office called and said you'd be coming. We've got a room all ready for you." She glared at Heath, then said, "Your mother told me you dragged this poor girl all the way down Poplar's Bluff to get Sam. What's the matter with you?"

Seriously? "I didn't—"

"Don't blame him," Libby said to Eloise with one of her big grins. "I made it to the beach all on my own. I'm probably just a little tired."

Eloise didn't look so sure. "Just to be safe, let's let the doc have a look at you. Can't be too cautious when there's a little one involved." After another pursed-lip glare in Heath's direction, the receptionist ordered Heath to stay in the empty waiting area while she wheeled Libby off to an exam room.

For the longest time, Heath just sat there, staring at the overly fussy floral wallpaper.

He picked up a tattered copy of *People*. But the last thing he was interested in was some starlet's issues with drugs.

A good ten minutes later, Eloise returned. "Libby sure is a pretty little thing. Seems like she has a real sweet spirit."

"Yeah." He feigned renewed interest in his magazine.

Ten more minutes passed, then thirty.

He checked on Sam. Found the temperature in the truck still pleasant and the dog lightly snoring.

Back in the waiting area, Heath wasn't sure what to do with his arms and legs. He felt all squirmy—like a little kid forced to sit too long on a church pew.

What was going on back in that exam room? Was Libby all right? Had she really hurt herself and the baby? If so, was it his fault? He should've insisted she stay up at the cabin with his mom. But then hadn't he told her to go back, and she'd ignored him?

Leaning forward, he rested his forearms on his thighs.

Honest to God, back when he'd been working, he'd waited out terrorists without feeling this tense. Even in the short time he'd known her, Libby had gotten under his skin. She had an energy about her—a spark, for lack of a better word—that struck him as pure radiance. For someone who had lived the past year and more in total emotional darkness, he was not only unaccustomed to being in the presence of light, but being around her physically hurt. It reminded him how much fun he and Patricia used to have, and how quickly that joy had been snatched away.

"You're sure you haven't had any spotting?" Kindly Doc Meadows asked the question while still making notes in Libby's newly made chart.

"No, sir. Other than being tired—and my back always hurting—I feel great."

"Hmm…" He removed his glasses, staring out the window at the clinic's parklike grounds. Not only was there a thick lawn, but there was also a garden blooming with riotous color and a meandering brick path that led to a gazebo. "Your blood pressure's slightly elevated, but the baby's heartbeat's nice and strong. We'll have to wait for your blood work and urinalysis to come back from the lab to have any definitive answers as to why you're fainting, but honestly, I think you're just plum worn-out. Do you have family you can stay with for the last few weeks of your pregnancy?"

Libby shook her head, though inwardly groaned. What should she say? Of course, she *had* family, but she wasn't ready to face them—not yet.

You make me ashamed to call you my daughter! Her

father's anger still raged in her head. *Go on, get the hell out of here and don't* ever *come back!*

The doctor sighed. "Pending no further immediate trouble, what I want you to do is get plenty of rest—and by plenty, I mean unless you're up for a shower or to tinkle, I want you off your feet. I hear you're staying with Gretta, and I know she'll take real good care of you."

"Thank you."

"You bet. But call if you experience anything out of the ordinary. Then we'll want to run you up to Coos Bay for an ultrasound and further testing."

"Sounds like a plan." A plan Libby had no intention of letting come to fruition. She couldn't imagine what that would cost, and she was already so deeply in debt to Heath and his mom that Libby wasn't sure how she'd ever see her way out.

"SHE STILL BACK THERE?"

Heath had been blessedly close to drifting off, when his meddling mother appeared in the clinic waiting room.

"Gretta Stone! Aren't you a sight for sore eyes." Eloise lumbered around the side of her desk to give Heath's mom a warm hug. Heath, on the other hand, got another squinty-eyed glare. "It's been forever since I've seen you."

"I know, I know," his mother said. "What with the motel's business picking up and getting ready for the Fourth, I feel like I don't have time to think, let alone breathe or play Friday night poker with my girlfriends."

"Well, just as soon as you steal the time, we'd love having you back. Clara Foster made the most incredible artichoke dip last week. You know how I've been going to the Weight Watchers meetings over in Coos Bay? Well, let's just say her dip ruined my whole week's points."

After both women laughed, then shared another hug, Heath had reached the end of his proverbial rope when it came to female small talk. "Eloise, don't you think you should check on Libby?"

"Heath!" Now, his mom was the one casting daggers. "Mind your manners."

Mind my manners? What was he, like, twelve? "All I want to know is if Libby's all right. She's been back there for over an hour. I've got Sam in the truck, and if it's going to be much longer, I need to—"

"You run on home, and get poor Sam settled." After patting his back, Gretta made a few motherly clucking sounds. "I'll take care of our little Libby."

Our Libby? When had that happened? They'd only known the woman barely over a day.

"Go on," Eloise urged, making sweeping gestures to send him on his way. "Your mom and I have this handled. Besides, I wanna hear firsthand what's going on with Hal."

Heath's eyes narrowed. "What do you mean? He has to find parts."

Eloise cast what he could only guess was a conspiratorial grin and wink in his mother's direction. "Oh— Gretta knows full well I'm not talking about car parts."

Both women found this hilarious.

Heath ignored them.

His mom's offer to deal with Libby's situation presented quite a dilemma. On the one hand, he'd like nothing more than to return to his cabin and stay there a month until he ran out of supplies. On the other, what kind of man had he become to abandon a pregnant woman? Especially since she might not have pushed herself hard enough to have landed up here if he hadn't been so short with her. Still, hadn't he done his part by delivering her to the doctor? What else could he actually do?

The decent thing—his conscience provided. *Like staying here long enough to ensure she's all right.*

Had he been on his own, he'd have growled.

"OH, GOOD." LACY CLAUSSEN, the nurse driving Libby's wheelchair, parked her in the reception room. "Looks like you have a couple options for getting back to the motel."

"Thanks," Libby said, pushing herself up, only to have the nurse give her a gentle nudge back down.

"You heard what the doctor advised. You get to be pampered. Let me wheel you to your ride."

"All of this really isn't necessary," Libby complained, but she was thoroughly weary. She suspected her forced smile failed to reach her eyes and even though she discreetly covered a yawn, exhaustion sagged her shoulders.

"Nonsense." Gretta slapped the magazine she'd been reading on a side table. "Let's get you home and in bed, and then I'll fix you a nice, hearty stew. You do like stew, don't you?"

Tears welling in her eyes, Libby nodded.

What was she thinking? Allowing this dear woman to continue caring for her when she had a perfectly good family a mere phone call away? Did that make her essentially guilty of duping these lovely people?

No. Eyes stinging from the effort of holding back tears, Libby promised herself that just as soon as she felt better, she'd work hard to repay every penny these nice people had spent.

"Aw, there's no crying in this clinic…." Eloise knelt,

wrapping her arm around Libby's shoulders, giving her a squeeze. "After a few days' rest, you'll feel so much better."

Libby nodded, but she wished she could be sure.

And then there was Heath, standing away from her and Gretta and Eloise and Lacy. He'd crossed his arms and backed against the wall. As usual, his expression was grim, but if she was reading him right, not in an angry way. If anything, she would've sworn he seemed…concerned?

"Let's get going." Gretta thanked Eloise, and Lacy wheeled Libby out of the clinic and into bright sun.

Heath trailed behind.

She wanted to thank him again for bringing her to the clinic, but while the nurse helped her into Gretta's SUV, he spoke a moment with his mom and then, shoulders hunched and hands crammed into his jeans pockets, he crossed the parking lot to his truck.

What was it about him that spoke to her? Was it the fact that they were both avoiding the past? Sure, she might accomplish this goal by forcing a bright smile through every rough patch, while he glowered his way through, but on some level they were kindred spirits in that they'd both essentially suffered a loss. He'd lost his wife. She'd first lost her parents, then boyfriend, then spirit—which was why she'd been driving home. To wag her proverbial white flag in her father's condemning face.

"Comfortable?" Gretta asked, jolting Libby from her thoughts.

"Yes. Thank you."

"Everything okay? You're missing your usual smile."

Libby flashed her new friend a half version. "Sorry, guess it's just been a long day."

"That it has." Gretta started the vehicle, placed it in Drive, then veered across the mostly empty lot toward the street.

It took every shred of Libby's willpower not to look back. At Heath. At Sam. At the strange connection she already missed.

Chapter Six

Libby was starting to feel like a broken record about telling Gretta and her brother, Morris, that their help wasn't necessary, but when it came to moving her few belongings from her motel room into the guest room in Gretta's personal home, they weren't paying her much attention.

"I think we got everything," Gretta said to Libby, whom she'd ordered onto a living room recliner.

Fred, Gretta's smelly bassett hound, wandered up to Libby, rubbing his snout under her draping hand.

"Where do you want this?" Morris stood at the front door with Libby's most prized possession—her potter's wheel.

Before Libby could even ask who'd brought it over from her car, Gretta directed her brother to the screened back porch. "Once Libby's feeling better, Heath thought she might want to wow us with her skills."

Heath had been the one thoughtful enough to bring her supplies? The notion that he'd cared warmed her through and through.

She hadn't done anything to deserve these strangers' kindness, but she sure appreciated it. "Gretta, I can't even begin to figure out how to thank you. Not many people would be so kind as to welcome a stranger, quite literally off the road, into their home."

"I'll let you in on a secret…." Gretta hefted Fred to a mound of quilts and chew toys in the corner, then collapsed onto the recliner opposite Libby. "Nothing makes me happier than rescuing a sweet stray from the side of the road. I found old Fred baying outside the elementary school. Somewhere around here are a pair of cats I found as kittens, hiding under a bush in front of the hardware store. When you first got here, though my heart couldn't help but reach out to you, I'm not naive to some of the ugliness that's out there in the world. I did a quick internet search on you—you know, just to make sure you didn't have an obvious criminal record—only to get a shock to find not only had you been arrested, but you also have a perfectly good family up in Seattle."

While Libby's heart raced, she could have sworn she actually felt the color drain from her face.

"You can stop looking so worried." Gretta flashed her usual kind smile.

Fred had left his appointed corner and now begged for Gretta to heft him onto her lap—which she did.

"I just, well…" Libby honestly wasn't sure what to say. She hadn't exactly lied to Gretta, but she certainly hadn't been a fountain of information.

"It's okay. As for your arrest, I abhor animal testing, and back in my youth, might've done the same thing. Now, in some cases, I suppose it's a necessary evil, but it still breaks my heart. As for the matter of why you haven't called your parents for help, I suppose that's for only you to know."

Libby sighed, covering her face with her hands. "The vandalism charge happened a long time ago. I got in with the wrong crowd, and thought we were just going to a peaceful protest rally. One thing led to another and one of the guys tossed a Molotov cocktail into a courtyard. Everyone was running and screaming and a few people were hurt. Police charged and dispensed tear gas. It was awful."

"I'll bet."

"As for my parents… Where do I even begin? Back then, my dad was mayor. Every time his reelection came around, he expected Mom and I to be part of his campaign. I was arrested during Dad's bid for a third term in office. His opponent used my actions against him, blasting the area with a smear campaign. You know the kind, 'If the mayor can't control his own daughter, how can we trust him to run our city?' The night of the election, after my dad's concession speech, the dark look he gave me…" She shivered. "In that moment, I believe he truly hated me. Mom, too."

"I doubt they *hated* you—at least from what little I know about you, you seem pleasant enough."

"*Pleasant* isn't exactly what they were going for in their offspring—at least my father sure wasn't."

"Got any peanut butter?" Gretta's brother popped his head through the kitchen pass-through.

"In the cabinet. But I'm making a double batch of stew, so don't eat three sandwiches."

"Yes, ma'am." The burly man with a thick head of salt-and-pepper hair saluted his sister using a couple slices of wheat bread, then ducked back into the kitchen.

"Sorry about that." Gretta stroked Fred's ears. "Where were we?"

"Nowhere. I shouldn't have said anything."

"You didn't." Heath's mom winked. "I did. And I'm

happy to let you hide out here for however long it takes you to get your car fixed, but after that you should go see your folks—not only for the baby's sake, but yours. I don't know the entirety of what happened between you, but maybe it wasn't as bad as you remember?"

SITTING AT THE kitchen table with her feet up on a neighboring chair, chopping carrots for Gretta's stew, Libby couldn't get the older woman's words from her mind. Could she have misread her father's harsh words and tone? No. But every year on Christmas, when she spoke to her mom, a piece of her shattered upon hearing the crack in her mother's voice. Libby missed her mom something fierce, but how did she just forget the horrible things her dad had said? Especially when every word had been true.

Mark my words. If you don't go to college, you'll end up pregnant, destitute and alone.

As if her father's words had been prophetic, Libby had become a knocked-up loser.

Gretta's house phone rang.

When she answered, Libby didn't mean to eavesdrop, but it was kind of hard not to when she sat five feet away.

"But Heath…" Gretta sighed. "You're being silly…. Of course Sam's important, but I think he'll be fine long enough for you to pop over here to share a meal." She winced as she tried to unscrew the Bloody Mary mixer she told Libby she used as her top secret base for her beef stew. "All right, but don't blame me if both of you starve to death."

Upon disconnecting, Gretta tossed her phone to the counter. "That son of mine makes me crazy. I can't imag-

ine what's gotten into him to make him even more an-
tisocial than usual."

Libby feigned intense focus on chopping her remaining carrots, but during Gretta's conversation, an idea
had crept into her head that now refused to let go. Was it
possible Heath wouldn't come to dinner because of her?

THE NEXT MORNING, Heath awoke to a hard rain and Sam
licking the underside of his palm.

Groaning, he eyed the dog. "Need to go out?"

A thumping tail told him his answer.

His grandfather had built the cabin with generous
eaves intended to keep the woodpile dry, but they also
worked as a dry spot for Sam to do his business.

The dog's hobble was slow, but his eyes had brightened and other than not being able to move as fast as he
liked, he looked none the worse for his adventure.

When Sam finished, Heath ushered him back inside,
changed his bandages and fed him, then helped him onto
the sofa.

When the dog cocked his head and looked longingly
outside, Heath gave him a rawhide chew he hoped would
keep him happy for at least a portion of the morning.

It was only seven, meaning he had way too much time
between now and bedtime.

He wouldn't have minded going fishing, but with Sam
out of commission, that idea was nixed.

Heath tried reading but couldn't get into the three-
inch tome on Afghanistan history.

A shower took five minutes. Dressing and brushing his teeth another five. Downing an energy bar and
sports drink killed another three minutes, according to
the glowing nightstand alarm clock.

Frowning, he grabbed his iPad, intent on at least catching up on national news, but the rain screwed with his already sketchy wireless signal.

He picked up his phone to see if it worked any better, only to see he had a message—no doubt from his mom. He was in the process of auto-deleting it when he noticed the number wasn't familiar.

Playing it on speaker, he got a jolt to hear the familiar voice of his old navy SEAL buddy Mason, aka Snowman—because he was from Alaska. "Yo, Hopper, did you fall off the earth? Nice job of keeping in touch, loser. Anyway, I've got vacation time coming, and Hattie's wanting to get out of town. Sorry for the short notice, but wanna hook me and my fam up for a few days' lodging over the Fourth? Assuming you're alive—call me."

Heath played the message again, just to be sure he hadn't dreamed his old friend's voice. Talk about a blast from the past. An unwelcome blast. Still, considering how many times Mason had saved his ass out in the field, the least Heath could do was give him a place to stay.

Sighing, he dialed his friend's number, made requisite small talk, arranged for Mason, Hattie and their three kids to stay at his cabin for the dates they would be in town, and in general tried to sound normal even though nothing could be further from the truth.

He was happy for his friend's newfound familial bliss. He really was. But that didn't make the cold edge of jealousy slicing his gut any easier to bear. Back when his fellow SEAL team members called him Hopper because of his knack for jumping objects while in a full-on run, Heath had believed he had his whole life mapped out. If only he'd known back then what a joke that would turn out to be.

Upon hanging up, he spent the next couple hours cleaning, welcoming the distraction from his thoughts.

But then, as he took a break to down a sports drink, another thought struck.

If Mason, Hattie and crew were at his cabin, where did that leave him? It'd be no big deal to bunk with his mom.

What *would* be a big deal?

Bunking with his mom *and* Libby.

"THIS IS SUCH a fun surprise." Two days later, Heath realized he hadn't seen his mother so smiley since her pickled eggs had won first place at the county fair. She held open her front door for him, stepping aside as he entered. "I'd give you a room at the motel, but with the holiday, I'm booked. Since Libby's in the guest room, that leaves you on the sofa—but you've always said it's comfortable, right?"

"Thanks." Had she been anyone but his mother, Heath would've snarled.

"Hey!" Libby called from the screened back porch that ran the length of the two-bedroom house. She sat in a low folding chair, legs spread wide with her pottery wheel between them. Her hands and forearms were coated with red clay, and she'd piled her pale curls into a messy, lopsided pile atop her head. Streaks of clay lined her cheeks and dots decorated her forehead and nose. Though outside rain continued to fall, her smile radiated light throughout the otherwise gray space. "How's Sam?"

"Conked out in the truck. I'll grab him once this rain lets up."

"Are you hungry?" his mom asked. "There's leftover stew. Plus, I made a nice chicken-and-rice casserole. Pineapple upside-down cake for dessert."

He couldn't help but groan with pleasure. As much as his mom drove him crazy, her cooking made everything better—if only for the short time it took to share the meal.

"I'm starving," he said, not sure what to do around Libby. She made him uncomfortable. She was too pregnant. Too smiley. And far too pretty for her own good—or, would that be his good?

"Sit with Libby." His mom pointed him to a lawn chair. "You two have a nice chat while I make you a plate."

Fred, never one to miss a suspected handout, stood and stretched from where he'd been napping alongside Libby's right foot to lumber after Gretta into the kitchen.

For a few awkward seconds, Heath wasn't sure what to say, but considering he still owed her for having found Sam, he cleared his throat, then noted, "Thought you were supposed to be resting?"

"This is restful for me. Nothing makes me happier than working with my clay. Thank you for retrieving it all from my car."

"Sure. It wasn't a big deal." He wanted to say more—*should* say more—but the honest to God truth was that the sight of Libby working her hands up and down the water-slick clay had pretty much left him speechless.

"I'm feeling so much better," she rattled on, "that I've made quite a few pieces, and your mom arranged for me to have a small booth at the holiday art fair."

"You feel up to that? It draws quite a crowd."

"I feel amazing." He believed it. Her skin glowed a healthy peach and her blue eyes shone brighter than they had in the short time he'd known her. "Maybe I'll even earn enough from sales to pay back you and your mom, plus have enough left to fix my car and be on my way. Because, even as sweet as your mom has been, the last thing I want is to be an imposition."

He liked the way she single-handedly carried the conversation. Took the pressure off of him. "Don't sweat it. I imagine Mom enjoys the company."

"Hope so." She went at it again with her clay. As much as Heath wanted to deny it, he found her actions erotic as hell—like a scene straight from the classic Demi Moore and Patrick Swayze movie, *Ghost*. He'd never admit to watching it, but as it was one of Patricia's all-time favorite movies, she'd watched it once a week near the end. It had brought her comfort—believing her soul lived on. Heath wanted desperately to believe, but the truth was, he couldn't get past his anger over her having been taken from him before their lives together had barely begun.

"Here you go." His mother presented him with a plate heaped with casserole—not that he was complaining. For the first time in…he couldn't remember when, he was starving.

"Thanks." He dug right in.

"When will Mason and Hattie be here?"

"They fly in on the red-eye tonight, stay in Portland, then drive down some time tomorrow."

"I'm excited to see those twins. And the baby must be walking by now."

"I suppose." What didn't she get about the fact that even if his old friends' kids were pole-vaulting, he didn't want to hear about it? Witnessing other people being happy in their marriages and lives only reminded him how meaningless his life had become.

A glance at Libby didn't help his worsening mood.

Couldn't she *craft* like a normal person? Did she have to draw in her bottom lip every time she stroked the clay upward, then exhale on the downward strokes? She made pot-making look downright obscene.

Sure that's not your own mind lowering her perfectly normal activity to the gutter?

He scowled all the harder.

"It's good you're here." Gretta plucked dead leaves from the fern alongside her chair. "I was just thinking how Libby's going to need some sort of booth arrangement for the craft fair."

"Gretta…" Libby's nostrils lightly flared as she curved her delicate fingers around the top of whatever she was making. "You're sweet for even thinking of it, but I told you, I can make do with the folding table that's in the backseat of my car."

"Why make do, when we have a big, strapping man at our disposal?"

"Mom…" Heath had finished his food and now took his plate to the kitchen.

"What?" Unfortunately for him, Gretta followed. "I was thinking we could use that old picnic tent I've got in the shed to keep Libby in the shade, then you could come up with some sort of shelving system with some of your father's lumber scraps he left piled up in the shed. I've got plenty of tables from the motel's banquet hall, but you'll need to run by Hal's to get the rest of the finished goods Libby has in her car—speaking of which, has Hal called you with any reports on the repairs?"

"Stop," he said under his breath. "I see what you're trying to do, and it's not going to work—no, more than that, it's ridiculous and downright embarrassing."

"What're you talking about?" She put foil over the casserole pan.

Still whispering, he snapped, "Whatever matchmaking thing you're doing with Libby. Give it a rest."

"Why would you ever think I'd want the two of you together? She's way too nice to be stuck with grumpy old you." After kissing his cheek, she popped the casserole in the fridge. "Since the rain's let up, why don't you bring in Sam, then see about that tent. It's been years since I've had it out, so it might need a good washing. I've got a few minutes so I think I'll just pop over to Hal's for Libby's things."

"Aye, aye, Cap'n."

His mother didn't look amused by his mocking salute.

Feeling like a fool for bringing up his matchmaking suspicions, Heath figured that ratty old tent wasn't the only thing needing a good hosing down. Had he imagined the fix-up vibe his mom had going? Why else would she be so consumed with helping Libby?

Is it such a stretch to believe Gretta actually cares about her?

No. But there was caring on a basic level, and then there was this whole scene his mother had set up where Libby was magically part of the family. When he'd plucked her from the middle of the road, he'd assumed she'd be in their lives for maybe a day—tops. Now, here it was Day 5, and she needed to go.

Why? Why did it even matter if his mother had made a new friend? Had he really become so selfish he begrudged his mother's happiness?

Heath groaned, covering his face with his hands.

Honestly, it wasn't his mother's happiness that was the problem, but the way being around Libby made *him* feel. He felt alive. And for a man who hadn't seen life in anything for a very long time, the sensation was akin to falling. And he needed it to stop.

Chapter Seven

Libby woke just past 3:00 a.m. with raging indigestion and an aching lower back. It felt strange helping herself to milk from Gretta's fridge.

Despite Gretta's kind, reassuring words, Libby couldn't shake her wish that she'd met the woman under different circumstances. Circumstances that didn't leave Libby feeling deeply beholden, with no immediate way to repay Gretta's many kindnesses. The same sentiment applied to Heath. Actually, everyone in town from Hal to Eloise to Nurse Lacy and Doc Meadows had been kind. How was it that these relative strangers treated her with far more understanding and compassion than her actual family—or even, her baby's father—ever had?

Eyes stinging with pending tears, Libby filled her glass, then returned the milk to the fridge.

Fully awake and miserable from head to toe, she shuffled to the screened back porch, breathing deeply of the cool night air. The grass must have been recently mowed as the sweet scent laced every inhalation. Crickets chirped, reminding her of the many nights she'd spent with Liam in their tent.

Looking at the past two years of her life, she couldn't begin to process where things had gone so horribly wrong. At the time, immersed in the happy glow of what she'd thought had been forever-love with Liam, sleeping outdoors had seemed perfectly normal. Now, as if viewing her recent past from afar, she realized how dysfunctional her relationship had been all along.

Sighing, she eased onto a patio rocker and managed to raise her swollen feet onto the ottoman.

The four vases she'd thrown after convincing Gretta she was healthy enough to do light work stood in a neat row along Libby's portable drying rack, barely visible by the light of the crescent moon. Alongside that, her portable kiln was all plugged in and ready to go.

She was pushing her luck to think her pieces would dry in time for the art show, but it felt good at least trying. Even after drying, they'd still have to be bisque fired and glazed, before firing them again. But considering her pieces sold for over a hundred each, if they did finish in time, and the show pulled a nice crowd, she'd be well on her way to repaying the many debts she owed all over town.

A faint jingling, and then footsteps on the brick walk, alerted Libby to the fact that someone approached.

Heart racing, she gripped the armrests, praying whoever—whatever—headed her way, was just passing through.

When the shadowy figure of a man paused in front of the screen door, her mouth went dry as she fought the urge to panic from fear of an intruder.

From outside she heard, "Damn it, Sam, calm down before you hurt yourself even worse. Fred, you need to hurry."

Moments earlier, adrenaline had surged through her. Now she felt flooded by calm and the curious sense of awareness that hummed whenever she and Heath shared the same space.

"Need help?" Now that she knew who stood outside, it was easy enough to guess Sam's condition had improved enough that he'd gotten tangled in his leash.

"Libby?" Heath opened the creaky screen door for Sam to bound through. Fred begrudgingly followed, only to collapse in a weary heap on the doormat. "What're you doing up?"

"Hey, cutie," she said to Sam, returning his enthusiastic welcome with plenty of petting and a hug. "I'm so glad you're feeling better." To Heath, she said, "I'm up because I feel like crap. What's your excuse?"

He actually chuckled. The sound not only surprised her, but warmed her. "Honestly, pretty much the same reason, but a different cause. You're probably blaming the baby, but I'm holding Mom's sofa responsible for my aching back."

"I'm sorry. Her guest room should be yours."

He shrugged, taking the seat next to her. "It's no big deal. The walk already worked out the kinks. How about you?"

Laughing, she said, "I have a feeling it's going to be a while before my back sees improvement—no matter where I sleep."

"Hang tight for a sec…." As abruptly as he'd appeared, Heath vanished inside the dark house, leaving her on her own with Sam and a now-snoring Fred.

"Where do you think he's going?" she asked panting Sam.

All she got for an answer was a wagging tail.

From the kitchen came a series of beeps, then the microwave's hum. What in the world was Heath doing?

She tried shifting in her chair, but no position felt comfy.

A few minutes later, Heath reappeared. "Lean forward."

"W-what?" He held something about the size of a package of Oreos, but she couldn't be sure. Maybe she just had a wicked craving for cookies?

"Humor me, and just this once do as I ask."

She did. And when he stood alongside her, she was surprised to find his masculine scent already familiar. He smelled outdoorsy, like the pines surrounding his cabin and briny sea spray drifting off the Pacific. His nearness made her hyperaware—even more off balance than usual. The flirty young woman trapped inside her wanted to giggle. The soon-to-be mother told her to keep herself in check. Nothing about her situation gave her a logical reason to crave anything more from this man than casual conversation.

"Let me know if it's too hot," he said, pressing something deliciously warm against her back. Instant pain relief brought on chills, then gratitude so complete as to knot her throat. Whatever he'd done, she was grateful.

"What did you put back there?" She touched the soft warmth, but still couldn't tell what it was.

"You'd laugh if I told you." His white-toothed grin shone in the faint moonlight. The baby lightly kicked, or maybe it was the sight of him that somersaulted her tummy? He was just so darn handsome.

"Promise, I won't."

"Okay, so back when I was a Boy Scout, we used to volunteer down at the old folks' home. Lots of them complained about aches and pains, but they couldn't use heating pads in their wheelchairs because they had to be plugged in. So Mom helped us make corn bags."

"Wait—this is corn on my back?"

There he went again with his supercute grin. "Told you you'd laugh. But yeah, it works great on back pain. My old roomies gave me crap about mine, but I was always catching them using it."

"I don't blame them. This feels so good I could purr."

"I'm glad."

She was, too. Since they'd first met, Heath had sent mixed signals. Always helpful, but also standoffish. Maybe for the rest of her time in Bent Road they could now at least be friends?

"All right, well…" He stood, crossing his arms, noticeably slipping back into his former distant self. "I'm gonna try getting back to sleep. You probably should, too."

"Yes, Dad." She winked, but he'd already left her.

Which made her sad.

Sam had stayed behind, though, and he wandered up, nudging his snout under her palm.

"That man's a tough nut to crack, you know?"

The dog wagged his tail.

Libby took that as a sign that when it came to her assessment of Heath, the dog agreed.

Fred, however, kept snoring.

LATE THE NEXT AFTERNOON, Libby wandered out to the yard to check on Heath, only to get a cold reception.

"Thought you're supposed to be resting?"

"I am." Libby ignored the perma-scowl that'd taken up residence on Heath's handsome features, culminating in a furrow between his brows. "But I made a few more vases I needed to set on the drying rack. Since I'm up, I figured I'd see if you need anything. Water? A snack?"

"Thanks, but I'm good." He'd been outside most of

the day, jury-rigging the picnic tent that'd been in worse shape than his mother had anticipated. "And you need to sit. Last thing I need is for you to topple over again."

"Are you this bossy with everyone, or just me?"

He sighed. "Really?"

"It's a legit question, Heath. I'm sorry if this project is an imposition. If you didn't want to do it, why didn't you just tell your mom 'no'?"

After setting down the hammer he'd used to drive two hollow aluminum posts together, he rolled his shoulders, looking anywhere but at her.

Sam, not fazed by his owner's gloomy demeanor, rolled onto his back, wagging his tail while partying in the grass.

Fred observed his hyper doggie companion with great disdain.

"Look—" Heath got back to work "—I don't have a problem building you a tent. I'm glad to do it. I just have a lot on my mind, all right?"

"Like what?"

"You asked me if I was bossy with everyone, well turnabout's fair play. Are you this nosy with everyone?"

She couldn't help but laugh. "Actually, yes. Now, is there anything I can do to help?"

"Can you hand sew?"

Nodding, she said, "Nothing fancy, but I know the basics."

"Great. If you'll sit, I'll bring you a project. Deal?"

"You don't have to talk down to me as if I'm a child."

He clamped his hand over his mouth as if he wanted to say something, but held himself in check. He even went so far as to turn away from her, but then he turned back. "From the day I first saw you, even you have to admit, you've been a straight-up mess. So can you cut me some slack for wanting to keep you in one piece until your baby pops out?"

"*Pops out?* Could you be any more insensitive?"

"Lady, you'd be amazed by what I can do." Though she was 100 percent sure he hadn't intended any naughty connotations, the part of her that hadn't had a decent kiss in months zoned in on the double entendre behind his words.

Face flushed, she looked away.

"You know what I mean."

Yes, unfortunately, she did. But her apparently filthy mind preferred her own special interpretation of his words!

But wait a minute… If he'd asked the question, didn't that imply he'd thought the same dirty thing as her?

"WHAT BEE CRAWLED in your bonnet?"

"Huh?" Ten minutes later, finally Libby-free in his mom's shed, Heath looked up to find his uncle. Could this day get any worse?

"You're banging around in here loud enough that I heard you all the way up at the diner."

"Sorry. Guess I'm in a mood."

"Wouldn't have anything to do with a pregnant little blonde, would it?"

Heath groaned. Was he that transparent?

"Your mom says you've been an ass ever since Libby came to town. And don't you have old friends staying at your cabin? Why aren't you visiting with them?"

"Mason and Hattie aren't due for another couple hours. They're stopping by for the cabin key."

"Good. Should we whip up a barbecue? I'm sure they won't feel like cooking after their drive."

"They won't be hungry." Heath screwed the side board into the base of the shelf he was making out of the scrap wood left from over half a century of motel and home repair projects. It'd be ugly, but maybe he could work magic with the gallons of leftover paint?

"How could you know something like that?" Uncle Morris grabbed a baby food jar his father had long ago filled with screws. "I'm in the food business, and everyone's hungry before, during and after travel."

"Is that a fact?"

"Proven. I see it every day at the diner." Right about now, Heath wished he'd told Mason he couldn't use his cabin. "And speaking of cooking, your mom said Libby's quite the baker. Did you know she made the apple pie we had for lunch?"

"Thought she wasn't supposed to be on her feet."

"Oh—she wasn't. Your mom made real sure Libby did everything from her seat at the kitchen table. What's her story, do you know?"

"Nope." And he didn't want to know any more than he already did. The fact that she was alone and pregnant was just plain wrong. What kind of man abandoned a woman he'd knocked up? Let alone his own child?

"Your mom told me Libby comes from Seattle blue bloods."

"Oh?" She never mentioned that.

"Makes me wonder what could've happened with her family that in her condition she'd rather bunk with Gretta and you than in some big mansion."

No kidding.

"All I'm saying is that there's more to her than meets

the eye. You might want to ask her about it. It's been my experience that women like that sort of thing—talking about themselves."

"Yeah?" Heath let his uncle's advice flow in one ear and right out the other. Why Libby apparently wanted nothing to do with her family was none of his business. Although, he did wonder if, like her ex, they'd somehow hurt her, too. If so, why? Sure, she was stubborn as hell, but in some ways that could be seen as an asset.

"But back to our barbecue, what do you think? Ribs? Chicken? Burgers and dogs?"

"I'm not hungry." Come to think of it, every once in a while he had caught Libby with a sad expression. He'd chalked it up to indigestion or lingering bad blood between her and her ex. It had never occurred to him she had trouble with her family. As much as his mom and uncle drove him nuts, he also knew they were unconditionally there for him if ever he needed their help or advice. How alone must she feel, with no one on her side? "Did Libby say anything else about her family?"

His uncle feigned interest in another baby food jar, this one filled with tacks. "Thought you weren't interested."

"I'm not," Heath said. Only for some inexplicable reason, he very much was.

BENEATH A SKY streaked in orange, pink, violet and blue, Libby stood on the fringe of the impromptu pool party and barbecue, intrigued by the discovery of yet another new side of Heath. While Heath's friend Hattie and Gretta played in the water with Hattie and Mason's three-year-old twins, Vivian and Vanessa, Heath tended ribs on the grill, catching up with Mason, who held the couple's one-year-old son.

Heath's whole demeanor had changed. He stood taller, spoke louder and seemed to possess a confidence she hadn't before seen. Was he putting on a show for his friend? Or was he really all of the sudden this self-assured?

Sam and Fred stood alongside the grill, both on alert in the event a rib accidentally fell into their waiting mouths.

"Libby!" Gretta called from the pool. The water was heated and steam rose, making an eerie scene with the glowing lights. "Join us! The water's bathtub warm!"

"I would," Libby lied, "but I don't have a suit." She was already self-conscious enough about her huge belly, no way did she plan on baring more than an inch of unnecessary skin. "I'll go help Morris in the kitchen."

"No, you won't! You're supposed to be resting. At least come dip your feet in the water."

Knowing Gretta wouldn't easily give up, Libby made her way to the pool stairs. She wore a maternity sundress, at least sparing her the embarrassment of needing help to roll up pant legs. After slipping off her flip-flops and keeping a tight grip on the shallow-end handrail, Libby managed to lower herself onto the still-warm pool deck while immersing her feet in sinfully warm water.

Eyes closed, she happily sighed. "That *does* feel good."

"Told you," Gretta said.

"As usual," Libby admitted, "you were right."

"Of course I was."

Like human atoms, the twins rocketed from the pool to chase each other and a barking Sam.

Fred wasn't budging from the grill.

Hal, holding a can of beer in his hand, hopped in the deep end where Gretta bobbed in her cute one-piece. The way they suddenly had their heads together, laughing, as if sharing a juicy secret, left Libby wondering if the two of them might be more than *just* friends.

The twins squealed their way onto the swing.

Sam leaped up to join them.

"They're a handful." Hattie grimaced.

"They're also adorable," Libby said. "I see the resemblance."

Hattie's smile faded. "Actually, they're not mine, but my sister's. She died shortly after they were born."

Hands to her mouth, Libby said, "I'm so sorry. I had no idea."

"It's okay," Hattie assured. "I mean, not that it's an ideal situation—obviously, I wish my sister were still with them, but Mason and I love them like they're our own."

"But the baby is yours?"

"Charlie?" She grinned. "Yep, I gave birth to all nine pounds of the little chubster. I feel for you being this close to delivering. Do you already have your delivery plan in place?"

"Not really." That fact brought her indigestion raging back. "With any luck, my car should be fixed long before July 23, which is my due date."

"Oh, sure," Hattie said. "I can't imagine it taking that long for a simple car repair. You'll want to be with your family by then."

Gretta and Hal swam to the stairs. "We're going to check on Morris. He's supposed to be making potato salad, but he's been gone long enough to grow the potatoes."

"That's a man for you," Hattie teased, giving Hal a playful wink. When Hal and Gretta were out of earshot, Hattie said, "Where were we? Oh—you were telling me about your family."

Once Gretta left, Libby wasn't sure what to say. She didn't want to be disrespectful to Heath's friend, but she also didn't want to launch into her depressing life story.

After a few awkward minutes, Hattie asked, "Did I just stick my foot in my mouth? It's kind of a specialty of mine, so if I did—sorry."

"It's okay." Rubbing her belly, Libby said, "I do need a plan for delivery, but until my car's fixed I'm kind of in limbo."

"Sure. I understand. Lucky for you, your car couldn't have broken down in a better place. The first time Mason brought me and the girls out here was not too long after Patricia's funeral. You do know about him losing his wife?"

Libby nodded.

"Well, it was a really horrible time. Heath was in his own death spiral and no one could snap him out of it. When his commanding officer gave him the boot, and Heath came out here, about a month later, Mason and I flew out to check on him. Once we saw how pretty and peaceful Bent Road is, we understood why this was the best place for Heath to heal. Patricia was an interior designer. She carried herself with this sort of Grace Kelly elegance I always envied. Everything about her was perfect. Clothes, hair, makeup, body, complexion—flawless. And the worst thing was that she was also really—I mean, *really*—sweet, so you couldn't hate her."

Libby's gaze strayed to Heath. *So that's the kind of*

*woman you loved. No wonder you want nothing to do
with a stray like me.*

"When she died, our circle was seriously scared for
Heath. He retreated further and further inside himself,
until he couldn't even properly do his job. The day his CO
handed him his walking papers was hard on the whole
team. They all tried getting his mind off of his loss, but
nothing worked. We SEAL wives are pretty close, and I
suppose the real kicker to all of this is that we're a tough
bunch, constantly forced to deal with the reality that one
day any of our husbands could leave for work, only to
never come home. All the guys have plans in place—you
know, in case the worst ever happens. No one in a million
years could've predicted Patricia would be first to go."

"That's so sad...." As if he'd somehow known they
were talking about him, for a split second, Heath met
Libby's stare before she sharply looked away.

"What's even worse is what's become of him since.
Obviously, he'll never find anyone as perfect for him as
Patricia, but surely there's a nice woman out there somewhere who would not only take care of him, but convince
him he's too young to just give up."

"Yeah...that would be amazing." How many times had
she wished for the same—to be with a man who loved
her and cared for her as much as she did him—only to
have ended up with a cheating creep like Liam?

"Gosh—" Hattie smacked her forehead "—how in-
considerate am I? Going on about poor Heath when I
didn't even think to ask about why you're pregnant and
on your own. Do you have a handsome sweetie worried
about where you are?"

Unable to speak past the knot in her throat, Libby
shook her head, then stood, making a mad dash for the

house. Or, more specifically, the privacy of her room. Hattie seemed like a genuinely nice person who, in another life, Libby may have welcomed as a friend. But right now?

She couldn't bear revealing to one more person just what a mess her life actually was.

Chapter Eight

"Where'd Libby run off to?" Heath asked Hattie while Mason took the ribs from the grill.

"Not sure. She dashed out of here the way I used to when I was carrying this guy and needed a restroom." She gave baby Charlie a jiggle.

"Mom-ma!" the kid said with a smile that made Heath's heart ache. Is this the stage of life he and Patricia would've been at?

"I know," she said in a playful tone to Charlie, who'd fisted a wad of her long hair. "Momma's hair's exciting, isn't it? But please don't pull so hard."

"That's my boy." Mason gave his son a quick peck on his chubby cheek. "Already SEAL strong. But do take it easy on your gorgeous mother."

"Aw…" With their son squeezed between them and daughters chasing poor Sam all around the yard, Hattie and Mason kissed, in the process displaying far too much tongue for Heath's liking.

"Geez, guys, get a room."

"Don't be a hater," Mason said with a wag of the meat tongs. "Where should I put the ribs while I'm grilling the sausage?"

"Set 'em in there." Heath pointed toward what his

mom called an "event hall" in her motel brochures, but was essentially a big room with lots of tables and chairs, a kitchenette, restroom and karaoke machine.

"Will do."

With his friend out of earshot, Heath asked Hattie, "Think you could maybe check on Libby?" he suggested, not wanting to seem as if he cared about her welfare, because he didn't—at least not in any way that mattered. Of course, he wished her healthy, but that was the extent of his concern.

"Why don't you?" Hattie was back to jiggling the baby. "I'd feel awkward—especially since now that I think about it, I'm afraid it was something I said that might've made her bolt."

"Hattie…" Weren't women supposed to know better than to run around upsetting pregnant women? Like, wasn't there a secret code about that sort of thing?

She winced. "It just slipped out, but I did ask her for the whereabouts of her baby daddy."

"Why? It's none of your business."

"Lighten up. It was an innocent enough question. And anyway, what does it matter to you? She's just staying over a couple days till she gets her car fixed. You'll never see her again."

"You're a mom. Since when did you become so insensitive?" He couldn't fathom why, but Heath found the notion of Libby leaving deeply troubling. Granted, she was too bright a light to be in his life, but to every so often have a fleeting taste of life's potential might not be all bad.

"You're a SEAL. Since when do you give two shits about anything remotely touchy-feely?" Only just realizing she'd cursed in front of the baby, she covered his little ears. "Earmuffs, sweetie. Momma didn't mean the bad word, but she spends too much time around sailors and she forgot how Uncle Heath sometimes makes her crazy."

"Whatever." After squeezing Charlie's sneaker-clad foot, Heath said, "Don't you believe a word of what she says, little man. Your mom's the true nutcase." To Hattie, he said, "Guess I'd better do damage control."

Heath wound his way through the ever-increasing crowd—a few of his mom's motel guests and Friday night poker group had joined the party, as well as Eloise, Doc Meadows, and even Hal and his two sons, who'd no doubt smelled the ribs' sweet sauce all the way from the garage.

Just past the pool deck, Heath did a double take.

Hal was slow dancing with Heath's mom to the country music playing over Gretta's newly installed outdoor sound system. Wait—*slow dancing?* The thought of his mom and Hal together, as in a couple, was too much for him to add to his already full plate. Surely he'd misread the situation, and they were just friends?

"How's Libby's car coming?" he asked Terryl on his way past, just to be polite, not to mention get his mind off the possibility of their respective parents hooking up.

"Not so good. Every part we need's out of stock. Thought we found one in Italy, of all places, but turned out it was the wrong year."

"Sorry to hear it." Heath was already heading for the house, antsy to make sure Libby was okay. "Help yourself to food and beer. We've got plenty of both."

To avoid meeting anyone else, Heath ducked between two cabins, then stuck to the tree line for the rest of the short trek to his mom's house.

His pulse raced from worry. How could Hattie have been so rude? No—downright cruel. Why would she have brought up such an obviously sore subject?

Slow down there, man. First, how could she even know it was a taboo topic? And second, aren't you taking this a bit too personally?

Yes, but it was important for the baby that Libby remain calm. Hattie had no business messing up Libby's happy vibe.

Finally in the house, he'd expected to find Morris in the kitchen, but his uncle had apparently finished, meaning he and Libby were alone.

He found the guest room door closed, so he knocked, then shoved his hands in his pockets, suddenly not so sure this was a good idea. After all, if he wanted to stay emotionally detached from the woman, shouldn't he have hung out with the rest of the group?

"Y-yes?" Libby's muffled voice sounded raspy. Was she crying? Why hadn't Hattie kept her big mouth shut?

"Hey, it's um, me—Heath." He pressed his palm to the door. "We're probably gonna eat soon, and I, well, just wanted to make sure you get to the table. You know, in case you're hungry."

"Thanks."

"Sure. So can I help?" *Because if you're crying, you might need someone to talk to.* Not that he was any kind of expert on hurting. But then, wait a minute, yes, he damn well was. When it came to missing someone, he could have written the proverbial book.

"Y-you mean help me find food?"

"Well, that…and, you know, anything else you might need help with." He'd pressed his ear to the door and heard rustling. What was she doing? Was she on the bed? Was her back hurting again? If so, he'd be happy to warm the corn bag.

Shut up! Could you be any more pathetic? She appar-

ently doesn't need help. Leave her alone. The sooner he ate his own supper, the sooner he and Sam could head back to the cabin.

Only too bad for him, Heath remembered his cabin was temporarily no longer his.

Sighing, he decided to switch courses. Instead of being vague, he'd be honest. "Look, Hattie told me she brought up your ex and you seemed upset. I'm really here to make sure you're all right—you know? Like, in your head?"

He might've heard her sniffle but couldn't be sure.

But then there was shuffling, and maybe footsteps.

And then he felt like the world's biggest creeper when she opened the door and he damn near fell into her room from having been caught off guard while leaning on her door.

"Sorry." She swiped fresh tears from her cheeks. "I didn't realize you were there."

"It's okay," he muttered, feigning interest in the door frame. "I was, ah, just checking to make sure you were alive."

"Sure. Well…" She gestured for him to follow her into the room. She sat on the foot of the bed. "I'm fine."

"Good. I know it's hard—talking about your past relationships with outsiders. It's bad enough talking about my wife with my mom or uncle. But strangers…" He shook his head, wishing he possessed more innate eloquence but hoping she'd managed to at least get the gist of his meaning. That he cared.

Never a fan of the dainty rocker that was the room's only chair, he sat next to Libby on the foot of the bed.

She looked as though she was about to say something, but then launched into full-on tears.

At first he wondered if it would be best if he left, but

then his heart went out to her, and he slid closer, pulling her into a hug. "It's gonna be okay," he said, too late realizing he was lying through his teeth. For him, even well over a year later, he still mourned his old life. Nothing would ever be the same. But maybe for Libby, since she'd at least have her baby to keep her company, things might be different? Better?

"I—I'm sorry for flipping out on you l-like this," she finally managed. "B-but when Hattie kept rambling on about how amazing your Patricia was—beautiful and kind and smart and talented and gorgeous—well, I got to thinking about how I wasn't any of those things. And h-here I am, carrying Liam's baby and even he doesn't find me d-desirable, then I guess I'm d-destined to spend the rest of my life a-alone and m-miserable...." Upon making that realization, she sobbed all the harder.

"Libby, no." Heath hugged her for all he was worth. "That's not true at all. You're crazy talented. I've never been much of a pottery guy, but your vases and bowls are pretty cool. Anyone could tell it takes a lot of skill to make them. And as for Liam not finding you desirable, well..." Gripping her shoulders, he nudged her back just far enough to meet his gaze. "He's a fool, because I think you're adorable."

"Y-you do?" She sniffled, then peered up at him with her pretty blue eyes looming impossibly large on her heart-shaped face.

"Of course. How could any man not find you attractive? You're sweet and funny and thoughtful. Any guy in his right mind would think you're a serious catch."

"R-really?" She was still staring, and the intensity in her eyes caused him to forget to breathe.

Since he couldn't speak, either, he just nodded. For some

reason he was fascinated by her sweet smell—watermelon and strawberries and snapdragons and summer-night air all rolled into one intoxicating fragrance he couldn't get enough of.

"B-because I think you'd be a good catch, too. N-not for me because I'm carrying another guy's baby. But if you ever thought you might…"

He couldn't fully focus on her words because as she spoke, she drifted closer and closer until her warm breath tickled his lips. His lonely lips. Lips that'd been so long without comfort or warmth they'd forgotten the simple, heady pleasure of pressing against…

She leaned closer.

As did he.

Closer.

Closer…

And then he wasn't sure how, but they were kissing, and he closed his eyes and groaned, slipping his hand under the curtain of her riotous hair. She tasted even better—sweeter—than she smelled, and he couldn't get enough, as if she was some kind of forbidden nectar.

She fisted the front of his shirt, making sexy mewing noises that made him instantly rock hard.

All thought gave way to raw sensation and pleasure and the certain knowledge that he was falling, falling and he didn't care. The only thing that mattered was making this pleasure last forever.…

"Heath? Libby? Are you two in here? Supper's ready!"

As if slowly waking from a dream, Heath opened his eyes to find himself staring into Libby's dazed expression. Her cheeks were still tearstained. Her lips now kiss-swollen.

"Heath, hon?"

Libby jolted back, eyes wide, pressing her hands to her lips. "I'm so sorry. I didn't—"

"Lord, me, too. I—"

"It was a mistake," she said.

"Yes. A mistake. These things just happen, right?" Which was why his heart uncomfortably raced and his stomach knotted. Because he needed a logical reason for having not only done the unthinkable—*unforgivable*—when there was none.

After a series of hitched breaths, she managed a nod.

"There you are," his mother said, entering the room. "What're you doing? Why aren't you at the party?"

"I—I wasn't feeling well…." Libby's curls were a mess. Had he done that? If so, he couldn't remember. In fact, much of the past few minutes were a blur, save for the humming awareness of her still lingering on his lips. And the shame.

Patricia, I'm sorry. It won't happen again. I promise.

"S-so I came back here for a rest. But then Heath stopped by for a visit and…"

"My Heath? *Visiting?*" Laughing, his mom stepped closer, making a production out of checking him for a fever. "Ouch! He's burning up. Chatty Heath is a sure sign to call an ambulance."

Lips pressed tight, Heath willed his pulse to slow.

The kiss had been just one of those things that didn't mean anything. That's all.

"Well, you both look healthy enough to me." His mom grabbed them both by their wrists. "Come on. Let's get back to the party before Hal, Terryl and Darryl eat us out of house and home. You know how much Hal loves a nice, hearty plate of ribs."

No, actually, he didn't. Their dance flashed into his

mind's eye. "Is something going on between you and Hal that you're not telling me?"

"Don't be silly. We're old friends." She dropped his hand to help Libby onto her feet. "You're all flushed. Sure you feel up to walking? Heath could make you a plate and bring it back here…?"

"I feel fine." She forced a smile. "Let's eat."

Heath said, "You two go ahead. I'll be right there."

"Why can't you walk with us?" his mother pressed.

"I need to make a call."

Hands on her hips, Gretta asked, "Who would you be calling? Everyone you know is here."

"Mom…" He hoped his back-off look conveyed the full extent of how much he needed a few minutes alone.

"Okay, okay…I can take a hint. Come on," she urged Libby. "For whatever reason, let's give him a few minutes alone. Men. As long as I live, I'll never figure any of you out." After a dramatic eye roll, she was finally gone, blessedly taking Libby along with her.

Since the entire room smelled of Libby's sweetness, reminding him of her light, and the way she'd made him not only forget his pain but once again feel whole, if only for an instant, Heath retreated to the back porch to be alone.

But there he was accosted by her pottery wheel and kiln. And the memory of her clay-slick fingers working the wet, raw material.

Only when he was outside did he feel capable of drawing a full breath.

And only when he was a half mile down the well-worn trail his mother and Fred used for their morning walks did he feel even remotely back to his normal gloomy self.

Leaning against the trunk of a massive Douglas fir,

he closed his eyes, willing Patricia's image to come. He needed to recall *her* smell, *her* taste. But when he needed her most, he found that no matter how hard he tried, his memories of her had faded.

The notion enraged him. So much so that he lashed out at the tree until his fists were a bloody mess and tears of long-held grief finally escaped him.

LIBBY TRIED ACTING normal at the party, but how could she when her every thought centered around Heath's kiss?

How had it happened? Why? What had possessed her to press her lips to his? Or had it been the other way around and he'd kissed her? How was she supposed to remember when every nerve in her body still felt hyper-aware of the moment they'd finally touched.

"Want more potato salad?" Darryl asked. Or was it Terryl? Even under normal circumstances, she could never keep them straight.

"That's plenty, thanks."

"Want a brownie?"

She shook her head. "You're a doll to offer, but I'm not that hungry."

Hattie and Mason and their three adorable kids shared a table with Morris and the redheaded fisherman she'd met in the motel lobby her first night in town.

"You should be starving," Darryl rambled on. At least she assumed it was Darryl due to the Dodgers cap. "When my cousin was in your condition, she ate anything that wasn't nailed down—that is, assuming it was salty or sweet. She hates vegetables. Dad brought a couple dozen doughnuts for the shop right before her baby was due, and I swear she ate darn near the whole box—cardboard included."

"That's a lot of doughnuts," Libby said with a half smile. *Heath, where are you? Why do I get the feeling you're avoiding me like Darryl's cousin avoids broccoli?*

"Yeah, she did that with our Halloween candy, too."

When Darryl launched into a new story, she politely commented here and there, but couldn't entirely focus. She needed to find Heath, talk over what had happened and reassure him nothing like that would ever happen again.

Are you sure that's what you want?

The voice came from out of nowhere and rocked her to her core. *Of course,* that's what she wanted. She was weeks away from becoming a single mother. The only thing she needed to focus on was her baby and earning enough money to fix her car. After that, she'd eventually need to reconcile with her parents. Nowhere in any of that did canoodling with a brooding widower have a place.

Then why are your lips still tingling?

Chapter Nine

By the morning of the fifty-second annual Bent Road Craft Fair, Heath's fists had healed from his stupid fight with a tree, and he'd turned avoiding Libby and his mom into an art form.

He'd been up early each day, either fishing the Umpqua with Sam or working in the shed on her display shelves. Each night, he headed back to the cabin to share dinner with Mason, Hattie and their kids.

As much as it hurt being around them, and seeing them reminded him of the double dates they'd all once shared when he'd been with Patricia, it hurt far less than dwelling on the guilt he felt about that kiss. But he also found himself more often than he'd like revisiting Libby's sweet smell and taste.

While ground-hugging fog still cloaked his mother's backyard, he skipped the formal breakfast Morris had served in favor of loading Libby's tent and shelving in the back of his truck. Then he took extra care to wrap her creations with bubble wrap before packing them in sturdy boxes.

By the time everything was good to go, he hoped breakfast was long over and his mom and Libby would be getting ready for the fair.

He couldn't have been more wrong.

Morris, his mom and Libby all still occupied the kitchen table and his mother was in the midst of one of her stories about him that made him look like a doofus.

"—so there we were at the San Diego Zoo when Heath decided he wanted to hug the bears. I nearly died, I was so scared. Back then, the enclosures weren't nearly as safe, and at four, Heath was a pistol. When he got it in his mind he wanted to do something, there was no stopping him. Well, he made it within five feet of the grizzly before a zookeeper could grab him, but the bear let out such a loud roar that Heath messed his pants!"

While everyone shared a nice, long laugh at his expense, Heath cleared his throat. "I've got everything loaded, so I'm heading to the park."

"Do you know my site assignment?" Libby asked.

"No, but it won't be hard to find someone who does." He grabbed a cinnamon roll and waved on his way out the door.

"Heath, wait!" his mom called. "Actually, you need to hold back a little because Libby's going to need a ride. You might as well go together so she can direct you on how to best set up all of her things. Oh—and I want you to take one of the back porch chairs and an ottoman, so she'll get plenty of rest in between sales."

Libby interjected, "Gretta, that's really not—"

"I'll grab the chair," Heath said, "but I'm sure she'd be more comfortable riding with you than in my truck. Besides— What the—"

Fred helped himself to the cinnamon roll Heath had held in his right hand.

While his mom and uncle exchanged belly laughs as the hound slinked off to his smelly bed to devour his stolen treasure, Heath could've sworn he felt the heat from Libby's stare, but he didn't want to risk looking that direction. As far as he was concerned, the less contact they shared, the better.

"Damn dog…" he mumbled.

"Watch your mouth," his mother reminded. "And you should know better than to leave food lying around."

It was on the tip of his tongue to argue that the roll had been in his hand, but he didn't want to lower himself to petty arguing over semantics regarding a dog. If anything, the incident just made him all the more ready for Mason and Hattie and their brood to head back to Virginia Beach, so he could get back to the solitude of his cabin.

"Okay, so back to our logistics issue," Gretta said, "I've got a few quick cabin turnarounds I forgot about this morning, so I won't be able to get to the fair until my guests are ready. Since Morris is needed at the diner, Heath, that leaves you to take Libby to set up her booth."

Swell.

"Sorry to be such a bother," Libby said.

"It's not a problem," he said, even though being trapped next to her in the close confines of his truck very much was!

By the time Heath drove past the fire station, Libby had had just about all she could stand of his silent treatment. "It was just a kiss," she said in her most matter-of-fact tone. "It'll never happen again, so you don't have to keep avoiding me."

"I'm not avoiding you. Why would I do that?"

"Seriously?"

When he managed a sideways stare, she stuck out her tongue at him.

When he couldn't help but laugh, she asked, "See? Was it so hard to share a civil moment?"

"No, but for real, that kiss was a straight-up mistake. I'm not sure what happened—don't wanna know. No offense, but for all practical purposes, I might as well still be married, and you're carrying another guy's baby. He could show up anytime and realize he made a mistake. You two could get married and live happily ever after."

Libby folded her arms.

"What? It could happen."

"And this truck could grow wings and a beak. Trust me, Liam's long gone. Besides, even if he could find me, why would he want me?"

"You need to stop with the whole self-pity routine." He pulled the truck to a four-way stop a block from the park where the arts and craft fair was being held. "The kiss was a mistake, but I meant what I said about you being talented and attractive. Hell, if circumstances were different, back in the day I'd have for sure made a play for you."

"Well, thanks, but while your flattery is appreciated, it isn't necessary. I'm secure in the fact that I'm a talented artist, but the whole pending single-parent thing has me spooked. I know Gretta told you some of why I left Seattle, but once I get back, for the baby's sake, I'm going to have to eat a buffet's worth of crow to get back in my parents' good graces.

"As for my eight-thousand-pound outward appearance, I doubt I'll win any pageants soon."

"Stop. That's what I'm talking about. You may not realize it, but you're beautiful—and I mean that in a strictly platonic way. You have this inner glow about you that's extraordinary—*really.*"

Her cheeks reddened from the intensity behind his stare. Had his eyes always been so green? His jawline so chiseled? He sported a couple days' stubble which made him look even more manly and rugged.

The driver in the minivan behind them honked.

Heath drove on, but not without shocking her by grabbing her hand and giving it a gentle squeeze. "I mean it. You're special."

"Thanks." She looked down, then back to him. Fragile morning sun tried breaking through the fog but ended up diffused and hazy, wreathing him in backlit perfection. At that moment she wished she was the kind of artist who captured scenes like this in watercolor or oils. That way she could keep him with her forever. Patricia might've died young, but she'd been lucky to have shared even a portion of her life with a man like Heath. Libby hoped she realized that while she was still alive. "I think you're pretty special, too."

He shrugged off her comment but couldn't hide the faint smile tugging at the corners of his highly kissable lips.

BY THE TIME Heath set up Libby's tent and she'd unwrapped and placed all of her pieces, he had to admit the setup didn't look half-bad. "We make a good team."

"Yes, we do. Thanks again for all your help. I can't believe how you managed to salvage this wreck of a tent— and the shelves are perfect. Nice and wide and stable. And I love what you did with the paint." He'd taken at least five different shades of yellow that the motel's shutters had been painted with over the years and colored each row a corresponding shade. When viewed from afar, it looked festive, yet in a classy, organized way—especially with the green canvas tent. Because of what he'd gone through with Patricia, he'd never consider yellow a favorite color, but making Libby smile almost had him forgetting the memories the color dredged up.

"It was my pleasure. Need anything before the crowd gets thick?" The fair, which would kick off the first day of the town's Fourth of July festivities, didn't officially open for thirty minutes, but there were already quite a few lookers passing by.

"I hate to be a pain, but a lemonade from the snack wagon would be delicious. And if a funnel cake happened to fall on what's left of my lap, that'd be okay, too."

He shook his head, but wore just enough of a grin that she knew he didn't mind too much indulging her cravings.

It'd been a month since her last show—a summer festival held north of San Francisco. At the time, she'd suspected Liam had been fooling around, and right before making a big sale, her suspicions had been confirmed when she'd slipped behind their tent for packing materials only to catch him making out with Rachel—a supposed friend who made fresh flower head wreaths. Though her creations were lovely with curled ribbons streaming down the back, Libby had found the woman's actions abhorrent. Everyone in their circle knew Libby carried Liam's child. How could Rachel be so cruel? As for Liam? His behavior was repulsive—especially so when he outright admitted to having been unfaithful more than once, then blamed it on her for gaining baby weight!

Libby had felt not only stupid for being the last one to realize everyone had known what was going on, but embarrassed and hurt and disillusioned by having thought herself in love with a man capable of such despicable actions.

It wasn't fair.

But then neither was the way her own father had treated her. Though he'd never been unfaithful to Libby's mom, his actions in expecting both of the women in his life to always accommodate his needs were no less cruel.

The fact that her most important relationships had ended disastrously didn't give much hope for her romantic future.

"Here you go, your highness." She glanced up to find Heath presenting her snacks with a silly flourish that was so unlike him she laughed.

"Thank you, kind sir. Would you like to share?"

"As a matter of fact—yes. I still can't believe Fred stole my cinnamon roll right out of my hand." He sat alongside her in the second chair Gretta had insisted he cart along.

"That dog eats like a pregnant woman."

"True."

They chewed in companionable silence, hands brushing while tearing off chunks of the sugary, fried cake. Every time they touched, Libby tried ignoring the achy awareness just being near Heath evoked. When he drank from her lemonade, she especially fought the memory of his lips pressed to hers.

For an instant their gazes met and locked before he hastily looked away. Had he felt it, too? The attraction that had no business being there, but was growing ever harder to ignore?

"Great day, huh?" After taking their trash to a nearby bin, he'd reclaimed his chair, stretching out his long legs, tilting his head back to catch the warmth of midmorning sun.

"Beautiful. Couldn't be more perfect. You wouldn't believe how many of these things I attend that get rained out."

"Oh—I remember a couple of years when this show has been chilly. We for sure got lucky."

She liked that. The fact that he'd used *we* in regard to the day. It implied he had an investment in the outcome. Maybe not so much monetarily—although, she'd certainly offer to reimburse him for expenses he'd incurred—but emotionally. Even though he'd avoided her ever since that kiss, apparently he hadn't been as detached from her as his actions had implied.

When the crowd grew thick and Libby actually made a few sales, Heath was on hand to help her wrap and pack customer purchases. He was there again with a turkey sandwich for lunch and more lemonade before she'd even realized she was thirsty.

As the sun rose higher, so did the temperature, and thankfully the tent Heath had refurbished kept Libby cool in the shade. That said, the longer she sat next to Heath, sharing casual conversation on topics ranging from her favorite foods to movies, the warmer her feelings for him became. Which didn't even make sense because the longer they were together, the more she realized how adept he was at carefully steering talk away from himself. Was it his company she was enjoying, or the novelty of someone actually caring about what she said?

She was on the verge of calling him out when Mason and Hattie arrived with their considerable brood in tow.

"This is stunning!" Hattie gravitated toward one of Libby's favorite vases. It was squat and chubby in shape, but the iridescent glaze lent it a whimsical flair. Hattie manned the twins' stroller, while Mason held squirmy Charlie. "Look, hon, wouldn't this be pretty on that little side table next to the entry hall bench?"

Mason wrinkled his nose. "Huh?"

"Ignore him," Hattie said. "I'll take it. And could you please pack it extra sturdy so it survives our trip home?"

"Will do." Heath handled the packing, while Libby handled the cash.

"You two make a good team," Hattie noted.

Heath grunted. "I'm only here because I have nowhere else to go since you guys invaded my cabin."

Though she was sure he'd meant his lighthearted statement as a joke, Libby feared there was a grain of truth to Heath's sentiment. Was he only here out of a sense of duty? To make sure she didn't overdo it?

If so, that not only hurt, but tainted the pleasure she'd found in the day.

When Heath handed Hattie her sturdy package, the women exchanged hugs and the guys shook hands.

Once again on their own, Libby was just about to voice her laundry list of concerns when a woman who'd looked over her wares at least four times finally stopped.

"Sorry to interrupt, but my name's Zoe." She handed Libby her card. "I run a gallery in Coos Bay, and if you have time, I'd love to talk with you about carrying your work. It's quite lovely. I've never seen glazing with such a luminescent quality. How long have you worked in the medium?"

"About four years." Was this a dream? Libby struggled to maintain her composure.

"Well, I've been in the art world forever, and trust

me, there are potters who've been at this decades who haven't got anywhere near your skill. Please call me."

"Thank you. I will."

"Good. In the meantime, I have to have this for my own collection." She'd selected a tall narrow vase made of three intertwining, vinelike structures meant to hold a trio of blooms. The primary glazing was yellow, but had a dreamy depth it'd taken Libby days to achieve.

While Libby worked in perfect union with Heath to complete the gallery owner's purchase and packaging, Zoe asked, "You two must be excited. When's your baby due?"

"Oh—" Libby reddened. "He's not the father. Just a friend."

"I'm sorry. Please don't—"

"It's okay," Heath said. "Honest mistake."

"Well, still…" She accepted her package with a nervous twitter. "Please don't let my awkward assumption prevent you from giving me a call."

"I won't," Libby assured.

"How great is that?" Heath asked once Zoe was out of earshot.

"Pretty stinkin' great." Head spinning—for once in a good way, as opposed to feeling faint—Libby sat down before she fell down from excitement. "I've never had validation like this—from anyone—let alone an industry professional." Cupping her hands to her tummy, she turned introspective. "My dad told me art was a waste of time. Liam said pottery was a dying art—if I really wanted to make something of myself, try water color or quilting."

"But what did our Libby do?" *Our* Libby? Heath shocked her by reaching out, softly stroking her hair.

His smile was equally as attractive as it was unreadable. Which only made her crave learning what made him tick all the more. "Exactly what you wanted, and look how it turned out. I'm happy for you. Mom and Uncle Morris— hell, damn near half the town will be, too."

"I couldn't have had such a successful day without your help."

He waved off her compliment. "All I did was wield bubble wrap and packing tape. You're the artist."

She still wanted to drill him on so many things, but now hardly seemed right. Not when for the first time in she couldn't remember when, she actually had something to celebrate.

"I HEAR CONGRATULATIONS are in order!" The moment Heath ushered Libby through his mother's back door, Gretta rushed from the kitchen to the screened porch to wrap her in a warm hug. "I'm so proud of you!"

"Thank you. It really was an amazing day. I made a little over fifteen hundred dollars, which means I can repay you for room and board and Heath for gas money and medical bills and all the supplies he bought for my booth, and hopefully still have enough left to fix my car."

"I can't speak for my son," Gretta said, "but as much as I appreciate your offer, I refuse to take one cent of your hard-earned money. Save it for getting home. I'm sure your parents will be thrilled to see you."

Libby paled. "I wish. Anyway, let me at least treat everyone to pizza."

"Too late." Morris held a pot in the crook of one arm, and nudged the porch's screen door open with his other. "To celebrate Libby's big day, I made spaghetti."

Long after their delicious meal and Heath had helped

his uncle clean the kitchen and Gretta had gone to bed, Heath walked the dogs with Morris and helped him close up the diner.

Back at his mom's, he'd selfishly hoped Libby would have also called it a night, but she sat on the back porch, reading.

The dogs were ecstatic to see her, but then he supposed he'd be excited, too, if she rubbed his belly and lavished him with praise.

"Those two worship you," he said. "They're going to miss you when your car finally gets fixed."

"I'll miss them." Was that a wistful note in her voice?

She winced when she leaned back in her chair.

"You okay?" he asked.

Nodding, she pressed her fingertips to her temples. "It's just been a long day—wonderful—but long. My body's one giant ache."

"Sounds like you need a good soak in a tub."

"Ha! As heavenly as that sounds, even if I fit, I'd never be able to get out."

An idea popped into his head. "While I was waiting for these mutts to do their business, I noticed steam rising off the pool. It's bathtub warm. Wanna soak in there?"

"I couldn't…"

"Why not?"

"For one, I don't have a suit. And two, what if someone saw me?" The way she looked down made him wonder if she was specifically concerned about him seeing her. Why? He'd always found pregnant women beautiful. She was no different.

"Sounds like a lot of lame excuses to me. We'll turn off the lights. If we're quiet, there's no way anyone would see us."

"I couldn't…"

"Chicken? Haven't you ever skinny-dipped?"

"Heath!" She pressed her palms to her cheeks, but even in the dim light he'd have sworn he saw her blush.

"What? It's fun. Come on…" He held out his hand. "I dare you."

Chapter Ten

"Don't look!" Libby whispered, praying none of the motel guests were up. Though it was nearly midnight, there was the odd chance someone could still be about. "I can't believe I let you talk me into this."

"Best as I can recall," he said from the deep end, "it wasn't too hard. How was I supposed to know you've never turned down a dare?"

"Lucky guess?" It was no easy feat removing her panties. Her bra proved even worse. It was the anticipation of escaping the awful pressure of the baby's weight, if only for a little while, that drove her toward the pool even more than Heath's challenge.

The cloudy night provided the perfect cover, and soon enough, she'd immersed herself in liquid bliss. Her formerly pendulous breasts floated high and she barely felt the weight of her belly. Pleasurable relief washed through her in waves. Was this how good she'd feel upon finally giving birth? No—even better, since her daughter would finally be in her arms.

"How is it?" Heath asked from barely five feet away.

"Better than sex," she said without thinking, immediately regretting her choice of words.

He laughed. "Damn, if it's that good, maybe you haven't been doing it right?"

"You're awful!" She splashed water his way.

"Me? You're the one who first mentioned the *S* word."

"Whatever." Eyes closed, she leaned backward into a float, relishing the night's inky cloak. The dark lent her a freedom she hadn't found in a long time, and she was determined to steal every trace of contentment.

The water's warm hold made her eyelids heavy, and before too long, she couldn't be sure if the heady experience was merely a dream.

Cool breeze licked her hypersensitive nipples, bringing on a yearning for the kind of man's touch that had landed her in this position.

"You really are beautiful."

"Oh—sorry. I didn't know you were there." Startled to find she'd unwittingly floated alongside Heath, she tried standing, but the water was too deep.

For a moment she floundered, but as always seemed to be the case, he was right there at the rescue. Only when her baby bump brushed against his bare six-pack, all manner of havoc coursed through her.

"Oh, my God…" he murmured, still holding her unnecessarily close, but she wasn't complaining. If she'd thought merely floating had felt good, being held by Heath proved a decadence beyond measure. She didn't dare breath for fear of him letting her go. "You feel so good."

He held her tighter still, nuzzling her neck, burying his face in her wet hair as if he were breathing her in.

His erection was no secret.

The humming awareness between her legs was most unexpected, and yet suddenly all-consuming.

In the water's warm, dark cocoon, they could've been anywhere in time or space, and when their lips met, it was by some unspoken yet mutual admission that whatever happened next, they were both adults and more than okay with it.

He kissed her like a man starved, and she answered his tongue's bold sweep, seeking to fill hungers all her own. For far too long she'd needed to be wanted, desired, and he made her feel all of that and more.

When she wrapped her legs around him and he entered her, it seemed like the most natural thing in the world. It'd been so long for both that neither lasted long, but long enough for mutual satisfaction to soon be found.

Finished, she sighed against him, resting her cheek on his strong shoulder.

"I'm sorry," he said, completely spoiling the moment. "I had no intention of doing that. It just happened."

"I know," she said, more for his benefit than her own. He was feeling guilty again. And she…well, she wasn't sure what she felt, other than regret that he was once again apologizing when what they'd shared had been special—at least for her.

Tears stung her eyes and as they drifted apart, she felt safe silently shedding them from a distance where he wouldn't be able to see. But then what would it matter if he did?

Obviously, what they'd shared had been nothing more than satisfying urges.

But if that were entirely so, why did her tears feel as if they might never stop?

"I'll grab a few towels," he said, already leaving the pool.

It was on the tip of her tongue to tell him not to bother,

but what would that accomplish, other than ensuring a cold, soggy walk to the house? "Thanks."

"I am sorry," he said upon his return from the utility room.

"Stop. Don't you have any idea how horrible that makes me feel? I mean, I know we don't share any real connection, but I'd like to think we're at least friends."

"We are," he said, holding out a towel for her to step into, while politely looking away.

"And you don't have to act as if the sight of a naked woman will turn you to stone, Heath—especially considering what just happened."

"Forgive me for trying to be a gentleman."

She snorted. "I think you've already missed the mark on that."

"So you're saying you didn't want to be with me?"

Sighing, she wrapped the oversize towel sarong-style around her. "That's not what I said at all. If you were truly concerned about coming across as a gentleman, you'd still be holding me in the pool."

"I can't. You know that. I'm—"

"No—don't you dare say you're still with Patricia, because point of fact, like it or not, she's dead. No matter how hard you brood or pout or wish for her return, it's not going to happen, Heath. Meanwhile, here you are, very much alive, obviously with just as many needs as the rest of us mere mortals, yet there you go, running off to pretend what we shared didn't happen. Well—newsflash—it did! And having you inside me felt wonderful and life affirming and I'm not sorry!" The moment the words left her lips, Libby regretted them.

Even more so when Heath pitched his load of towels to the pool deck, then yanked on his jeans, T-shirt and leather sandals before storming away. He didn't even walk toward the house, but headed to the road.

"Heath? I'm sorry!" she shouted after him. "I don't mean to sound cruel, but you can't go on living this way, pining for your dead wife. It's not really living at all."

He kept walking. He didn't so much as turn around to acknowledge her words.

Hugging herself, once again feeling gravity's crushing weight upon her pregnant body, Libby felt terrible about the hurt her words had inflicted on Heath.

Of course, he rationally understood Patricia was never coming back. But in his heart? She feared that may be an entirely different matter.

Heath ran all the way to the crashing shore. His lungs and thighs burned, but he didn't care. Nothing mattered except running from the pain caused by not only Libby's harsh words, but his own outrageous actions.

What had he been thinking?

Obviously, he hadn't been thinking.

But what was he supposed to do about it now? An act like this couldn't be undone. There'd be repercussions.

Even worse, he didn't get his cabin back until Mason and crew left on the fifth to visit family in Alaska, meaning Heath had three more days trapped in the same house as Libby. Or did he?

Sure, it was the height of summer tourism season, but that didn't mean he couldn't just pop a tent somewhere—anywhere—if it meant avoiding her.

Sure it's her you're avoiding, buddy? Or the way she makes you feel—not just alive, but good. Happy. Not remotely depressed. Even worse, when you're with Libby, you stop dwelling on the past.

Heath picked up a rock and hurled it with a mighty roar at the angry Pacific.

When would he stop feeling this way? When would he be able to forgive Patricia for leaving him and himself for not being able to keep his promise to her to never be with another woman?

The really ironic part about his situation was that Patricia never wanted this limbo for him. She'd made deathbed pleas for him to not only find someone else to love, but to live a life full enough for the both of them. She'd made him promise to follow through on all of their shared dreams—have kids and a great house. Take family vacations and grow old with someone while their children grew into adults and had children of their own.

Patricia had dearly wanted all of that for him, but in those agonizing moments when he'd watched life drain from her body, he'd wanted nothing more than to keep her with him always.

In those moments, he'd made his own promise.

I'll love you forever, he'd cried, holding her to him, refusing to let go until a nurse gently intervened. *I promise to never love any woman the way I love you.*

Sitting hard on the rocky shore, he planted his hands behind him for support and crossed his legs at the ankles.

Tipping his head back, he looked to the sky for answers, but heavy cloud cover only made him feel more alone.

"You slept late this morning," Gretta said when Libby wandered her way from the bedroom to the kitchen. "Feel better?"

I wish. "Great. Thanks."

"I was thinking, since yesterday was such a busy day,

you should probably use today to rest. So how about a nice beach picnic? Morris loves cooking over a campfire, and we could wrangle a few harrowing SEAL stories out of Heath."

Oh, have I got a story for you! "Um, that sounds nice, but let's play it by ear. I'm really not feeling up to much."

"Of course. I'm sorry. Here I am planning out your afternoon when you haven't even had breakfast. Would you like eggs or oatmeal?"

"I can get it. Please, go on with whatever you were doing. I'm pregnant—not an invalid." Libby didn't mean to be short with Gretta, but she just wasn't in the mood for hovering. Come to think of it, she wasn't in the mood for much of anything other than hiding under the covers until her baby girl decided she was ready to enter the world. "I'm sorry. Guess after all of yesterday's excitement, I'm feeling kind of blah."

"That's understandable," Gretta said, ushering her to a kitchen table chair. "But you still have your talk with the gallery owner to look forward to. What was her name? Zoe?"

Libby nodded.

"Maybe Heath can drive you to Coos Bay on Monday? It's a lovely area. You can make a whole day of it."

Yeah, I don't think that's going to happen.

For an instant, Libby closed her eyes, wishing Heath's angry glare wasn't the first image popping into her mind.

"I would take you myself, but with the motel fully booked I really should stay here. You know, in case we run out of towels or there's a plumbing emergency. And speaking of towels, I can't believe how rude some guests are. There's a metal bin near the pool that's plainly marked for used towels, yet I found at least five of them just tossed to the pool deck this morning. What's wrong with people these days? Were they raised in barns?"

Heat rose up Libby's neck, flaming her cheeks.

If Gretta knew the truth behind how those towels had been strewn, she'd no doubt suffer from an apoplectic fit.

"Will you be all right if I go throw another load in the washer?"

"Of course. Is there anything around here you need me to do?"

"Not particularly. Thanks for the offer but I'd rather you rest. You've had enough excitement for one weekend."

Wasn't that the truth!

"Oh—and when Heath wakes up, ask him about the picnic. I really think it'll be fun."

If your idea of a good time includes chilling with a morose, brooding, foul-tempered, miserable wretch of a man.

Just as Gretta left out the back door, Fred wandered over. He sat. Scratched a bit at his tummy, then plopped back on his haunches to stare at her expectantly.

"You think food solves everything, don't you?"

He barked.

She fished a few dog biscuits from the canister Gretta kept on the counter, then tossed them to the begging dog.

"Where's Sam?" Since Fred wasn't answering, Libby made a sweep of the house, only to come up empty. Not only was Sam not home, but neither was Heath.

Her anger with Heath morphed to worry when she found that the bedding Gretta set out for him every night had been left untouched. Had he been gone all night? Should she launch a search?

In her room, she dressed in maternity shorts and a

draping floral blouse, slipped her feet into sandals and ran a brush through her hair.

In the kitchen, she checked Fred's food and water bowl, only to find them both full.

"Hold down the fort," she said to the dog before creaking open the back door.

Outside, the day was far too pretty to suit her dark mood.

Why couldn't Heath just be a normal guy? Sleep with her, thank her for a good time, *then* leave? Why'd he have to storm off, making her worry about his emotional well-being?

Moreover, why couldn't she just let him be? Why did it matter how he felt, because it was obvious that after what they'd shared, he couldn't give two figs about her frame of mind.

But then why should he? For all practical purposes, as pleasurable as their union had been, it was essentially a one-night stand—not anything she'd ever imagined herself indulging in, but if she had to put a label on it, there was nothing else their impromptu hook-up could be called.

That said, she was deeply sorry for bringing up his obsession with Patricia. First and foremost of the issues she planned to discuss, that one topped her list.

When she'd shuffled her way around the motel's lot and found Heath's truck, but no sign of Heath, Libby decided to take her search further by borrowing his keys.

She'd made it to the house and back to the truck without being seen when Gretta emerged from one of the guest cabins with her arms laden with bed linens.

"Where are you off to?" Heath's mom asked. "And where's my son? I'd feel better about you leaving if you have someone to keep an eye on you."

"Actually—" Libby crossed her fingers behind her back for the fib she was about to tell "—Heath just called the house phone. He's with Sam, and they walked a little too far. He, um, asked me to pick them up."

"Why is he bothering you? He knows you're supposed to be resting."

"I'm feeling great." Libby hated lying again, but in this case it couldn't be helped. She not only needed to find Heath, but talk to him. And it wasn't a conversation Gretta needed to be a party to.

"If you're sure you're okay. But be back soon. Morris and I still want to try for an afternoon picnic. Oh, and when you grab Heath, tell him to invite Mason and Hattie and their kiddos. Just to be neighborly, I think I'll even call Hal and his boys."

"Sounds good."

Hattie had hauled herself behind the truck's steering wheel when Gretta shouted, "Libby, hon, wait up! You didn't even tell me where you were going!"

Vowing to ask forgiveness after she came home with Gretta's son, Libby pretended to not hear Heath's mom or see her chasing after the truck in the rearview mirror. Thankfully, the circle drive allowed her to make a clean getaway before Gretta could catch up.

Now the only question was, where did she even start looking for a man who obviously didn't want to be found?

Chapter Eleven

Not only was Heath hungry and tired, but Sam looked as though he was wearing down, too. Heath had believed he was alone when he left his mother's property, but apparently Sam was even smarter than Heath gave him credit for since the dog must have nosed open the screen door to follow.

"Right about now, I'm guessing you wish you'd stayed home, huh?" He rubbed behind the dog's silky ears.

Sam licked his hand.

It was one thing to run himself to his physical limits, but now he had the added guilt of worrying about his dog.

They'd walked quite a way down the shore, rounded a bend and had just made it back to the public parking lot when Heath groaned. "You've got to be kidding me...."

The lot was deserted save for one familiar truck. His.

Even worse, farther down the beach tottered Libby.

Lord...

He sharply exhaled, then swiped his fingers through his hair. He didn't know how to face her. He hadn't just botched their situation, but annihilated it.

Sam adored Libby. One look at her and the traitorous mutt found his second wind, bounding down the shore, barking the whole way.

While his dog and Libby shared a touching reunion, Heath regrettably knew what he had to do.

Facing her, bolstered by the rhythmic waves that had always brought solace, he blurted, "Sorry."

"No—I'm sorry." She wiped tears. "I never should've said anything about Patricia. It was heartless and cruel and mean-spirited."

He couldn't help but cast her a faint smile. "There you go again. All of those mean the same."

"Does it matter?"

"Nope."

"All right, then. Accept my apology, I'll accept yours and let's get on with our day."

Hands in his pockets, Heath kicked at the sand. "What if I feel like there's more to say?"

"Then say it. You're a grown man, Heath. You used to be a navy SEAL. Do you have any idea how amazing that is? You've seen and done things I can't even imagine—probably don't want to imagine—so I can't for the life of me understand what you're doing holed up in Bent Road, fishing or lounging around your mother's house when you could be off saving the free world."

Heath hung his head in shame.

Her words hurt, but he couldn't deny their truth.

"I know we hardly know each other," she said, "so maybe I don't have the right to say any of this, but on the other hand, your mother's so kind that I almost feel like she's doing you a disservice by not giving you an earful. Last night…" She flopped her hands at her sides. "It was hot. Beyond unexpected. And really, *really* great. The way you ran off, I got the feeling you're ashamed of what happened between us, but you don't have to be. You're a single, handsome man who acted on natural feelings. End of story. No, actually—"

"Okay, whoa." Hands to her shoulders, he held her at arm's distance so she'd be sure to face him while he took a turn at venting. "Everything you said is true. Me running away was the equivalent of slapping a Band-Aid on a gaping wound. I get that. My problem is figuring out what to do with this wad of emotions I can't seem to shed."

After releasing her, he took a step back, covering his face with his hands. "I loved Patricia like I didn't know it was possible to love. When I lost her…there were days I wished I'd died myself. When Sam was gone, I caught myself slipping back into that frame of mind."

"Heath…" She touched his forearm—barely—but it was enough to begin his unraveling.

"Please understand, I—I'm not suicidal or anything, but I don't know where to go, what to do. I'm lost."

"You're in luck, *lost* is my specialty. I've lived most of my life there." Her tone said her words were meant to be a joke, but the shine to her eyes told a different story. "I've been fortunate enough to have never lost a loved one the way you have, but my own dad kicked me to the curb like I was garbage. Liam, the father of my baby and man I thought I'd spend the rest of my life with pretty much did the same. So when it comes to loss, I consider myself a specialist."

"Yet you're always smiling. How do you do it?"

"Sheer will…" Her misty-eyed smile ignited a long frozen corner of his soul. "Because really, what's the alternative? Sure, I could curl up in a ball and cry night and day, but what would that prove? Especially, when I have so very much to be thankful for." Hugging the baby, she said, "I have a daughter on the way, and you and your mom and so many other great friends that up until a week ago, I never even knew existed. Then there was the craft show—making so many sales and meeting Zoe. As if all of that weren't enough, there was last night…with you. In my bed this morning, I pinched myself to make sure I hadn't dreamed it all."

"See? You have your baby to look forward to—your work. I have nothing."

Waving off his comments, she argued, "Okay, so you might not have a child on the way but, Heath, do you have any idea how much your mother and uncle love you? As for work, you're a SEAL. I'm not an expert about navy stuff, but seems to me that someone with your kind of training would be in high demand."

"I'm out of shape."

Hands on her hips, she pursed her lips and cocked her head. "Really, Heath? That's the best you've got for me? How long would it take you to get back into *shape?* Especially since you're looking pretty good to me." Her cheeks flushed adorably.

"I don't know…"

"How about this? You dared me to skinny-dip last night, so I dare you to at least call your boss or major general, or whoever's in charge of letting you get back to what you do. If he tells you to take a hike, then resume your busy schedule. But, Heath, what if he says he needs you? How amazing would you feel to once again be giving to others instead of sitting around replaying a tragic situation day after day that you have no hope of ever making better?"

LIBBY'S SPEECH STRUCK an anticipatory chord that stayed with Heath throughout the day. Could Libby be right? Did he have a shot at getting his life back on track?

He was grateful to her for keeping what had transpired between them confidential, meaning he could spend the sun-flooded afternoon picnic his mom had organized enjoying himself as opposed to standing around, feeling awkward—at least when his mom wasn't off flirting with Hal.

Stuffed from too many servings of his uncle's fried chicken, Heath sat in the sand beside Mason, who was building a sand castle with his girls. Like everything the man did, the structure was top-notch, featuring a moat, dragon and princess high atop a turret.

"You've got a great-looking family," Heath said.

"Thanks, man. Coming from you, that means a lot."

"Yeah?"

His friend gave him an odd, indecipherable look. "Yeah. I always looked up to you and Patricia. You two seemed to have it all figured out. When she…well, when she passed, none of us knew what to do for you."

"There's wasn't much anyone could do." He drew a pattern in the sand with a twig. "Which made it all the harder, considering we were in the business of solving any problem."

"My point exactly. We felt helpless. And for that, I'm sorry."

Heath shrugged. "I appreciate it, man, but what's done is done."

They sat a few more minutes in companionable silence, Mason helping the girls while Heath stared into the crashing surf where Sam frolicked.

Fred stared on disapprovingly from dry ground.

His mom, Hal, Libby, Hattie and the baby shared the picnic table, while Morris and Hal's boys chatted up a brunette down the shore. All in all, it'd been a surprisingly good day. Far different from how he'd expected it to develop in the dark before dawn.

Who did he have to thank for that fact? Libby. For a woman five years his junior, at times she seemed dozens of years wiser.

"Hey, Mason?"

"Uh-huh?" His friend was focused on flying buttress construction.

"Not saying I'm gonna do it, but what would you think the reception would be if I approached the CO about resuming my post?"

"Are you kidding me?" Mason rocked back onto his heels, brandishing a goofy grin. "He'd be thrilled. So would the rest of the guys. We miss you, man. But what're you going to do about Libby?"

"What do you mean?"

"Aren't you two an item?"

"No. Not at all." But if that were the case, why did his stomach knot at the prospect of his life moving on without her?

"Don't look now," Hattie teased, bouncing Charlie on her lap, "but a certain someone can't stop staring at you."

"He's just being friendly." Libby glanced up to find her gaze locking with Heath's. She smiled shyly before looking down, ignoring the flush of achy awareness flooding her system from the memory of their brief but hot encounter.

Thankfully, with Gretta and Hal in lawn chairs nearer the surf, immersed in their own conversation, Gretta wouldn't have overheard Hattie's comment.

Libby would be mortified if Heath's mom had so much

as an inkling of what had transpired between Libby and her son.

Hattie snorted. "If that's the look of a *friendly* man, then I'm about to be crowned Miss America!"

"It could happen," Libby mused. "You have gorgeous hair."

"Thanks, and you're sidestepping the issue. Spill your guts. Is there something going on between you two?"

Dear Lord, yes. Fanning suddenly flaming cheeks with a paper plate, Libby shook her head. "No, nothing like what you're hinting at, anyway. If anything, we're like squabbling siblings."

"Uh-huh…" Hattie leaned to the table's opposite end to dredge her pinky finger through the frosting on the chocolate cake Morris made for the occasion. "Thank the good Lord I never had a brother who looked like Heath—because well—" she laughed "—he'd be my brother instead of my boyfriend."

"Hey," Libby teased, "you've already got one great guy. No fair hogging them all."

"Aha! So you are admitting you like Heath as *way* more than a brother?"

"I'm admitting nothing." She sipped pink lemonade. "And unless you want to get on Gretta's bad side, you might want to assess that situation…" She nodded toward the cake where one of the twins was helping herself by tiny, chubby fistfuls.

"Vivian!" Hattie shouted. "You know better."

"Yum!" The chocolate-smeared cherub grinned. "Good!"

"See what you have to look forward to?" Hattie asked.

Hugging her belly, Libby said, "I can't wait." And she meant it. But as much as she looked forward to finally meeting her baby girl, she was that afraid of raising her all on her own.

"I don't mean to pry," Hattie said while cleaning Vivian's fingers—Vanessa still worked on her castle with Mason, "but you mentioned when we first met that you don't have a birth plan in place. What're you planning to do?"

Libby sighed. "As soon as my car's fixed, my only real option is heading back to family in Seattle with my tail tucked between my legs."

"I take it you don't get along?"

"That'd be putting it mildly. Long story short, when I was eighteen, my dad and I had the mother of all fights. He made ultimatums I knew I couldn't live with, so I didn't even try. I left home and never looked back."

"How's your mom? Was she supportive?"

"She tried, but she's old-school—believing her husband should be *obeyed*. When Dad sent me packing, she agreed it was for the best. For a while, I had a hard time accepting what I took as her betrayal, but now that I'm older, I see she probably felt like she didn't have a choice."

"A parent always has a choice when it comes to supporting their kid." Libby hadn't realized Heath had stepped behind her. How much had he heard? "What both of your parents did is unforgivable."

"Thanks for the support," she said, "but it's not that black-and-white. Back then, I was a wild child, and they're about as straightlaced as they come. Mom was thinking debutante balls while I was plotting tattoos and piercings. Thankfully, I grew past that rebellious stage, but considering some of the things I'd done, all of the money in private school tuition I pretty much wasted, I guess I'd be upset, too."

"It shouldn't be just about the money." Heath sat beside her, forced by the cooler on her right side to be close enough for their shoulders, forearms and thighs to brush. She tried playing it as no big deal, but her pulse raced as fast as the twins chased barking Sam. "You're their daughter. No matter what, they should accept you for who you are."

Even after they'd all shared cake and laughter when Vivian and Fred slinked off with the leftover corn on the cob, Libby struggled to get Heath's words from her mind.

When she finally became a mother, she hoped to share his high ideals, but she also wasn't naive enough to believe all parenting situations would be easy.

On the ride home, Libby shared the truck's seat with Sam and Fred. Heath drove, and she couldn't help but admire the color the day spent in the sun had left on his stubbled complexion. So much had transpired between them in the past twenty-four hours. Their lovemaking felt like a dream. His running off, and their squabble that morning seemed a million years away.

Where they were concerned, time seemed to hold no meaning. Even though they'd only officially known each other a little over a week, she felt as if she'd always known him. Moreover, she inherently knew she'd always *want* to know him.

"Have plans for in the morning?" he asked.

"Nope—unless Hal announces my car's done."

He snorted. "Back at the beach, Darryl told me they were waiting for parts from literally all over the world, so I wouldn't hold your breath on that one."

"Okay, so since I apparently have my day wide-open, what did you have in mind?"

He rubbed Sam behind his ears. "Thought we might wind our way over to Coos Bay. See about getting you a meeting with that gallery owner."

"Sounds good." She was careful to not let her voice betray the amount of excitement she actually felt at the prospect of spending her day alone with him. "But if I do that, you've got to promise me to call whoever you need to, in order to see about getting back to your job."

"Yes, *Mom.*" When he cast a wink and grin combo in her direction, it was all she could do to keep from swooning. Good thing the man seemed to have no idea how handsome he actually was, or she'd be in big trouble!

After a few more minutes' companionable silence, Heath cleared his throat and said, "Thanks again for this morning. I never talk about Patricia, and…" her heart ached to witness his eyes well "…it was time."

"You're welcome. Feels good to finally do something for you."

"While we're on serious topics, do me a favor and stop dwelling on any debt you think you owe me. I only did what any ordinary nice guy would."

That might be, but so far in her travels, Libby hadn't encountered anyone quite like Heath or his mom and uncle. They were lovely, remarkable people she one day aspired to resemble.

When the tires crunched on the gravel drive leading up to Gretta's home, happiness of the kind she'd experienced precious few times in her life flowed through her. It was probably hormones making her hypersensitive to the role her new friends played in her life, but that didn't detract from her overall sense of well-being.

And dread.

Because any day now, this illusion of having a true

home and family would be shattered with one call from Hal announcing her car was done.

"Sit tight," Heath said upon parking his truck alongside the shed. "I'll help you down."

"Thanks." Ordinarily, she resented needing his help, but in her current mellow state, she not only appreciated his assistance, but welcomed—craved—his touch.

Sometime in the past twenty-four hours they'd turned a corner in their friendship. It hadn't just been the making love that had solidified their bond, but an intangible something more she couldn't have defined if her life depended upon it.

When Heath lifted her from her seat, had she imagined his hands lingering longer than necessary on her torso, or the pads of his thumbs brushing the tender sides of her breasts?

"No offense," he teased, "but I swear you've put on twenty pounds since the first time I hefted you from the middle of the road."

"Did you just call me fat?"

He laughed. "Absolutely. And you have no idea how happy it makes me to see you with meat on your bones. When you first showed up, you reminded me of a scrawny kitten. Now..." He hastily looked down. He still held her, his thumbs still singeing the tender sides of her breasts. Her breath hitched in anticipation and hope of him once again kissing her as if there was no tomorrow. Because for her—them—there wasn't.

As soon as her car was fixed, she'd march into the proverbial lion's den to make nice with her parents and give birth to her baby. If Heath had a lick of the sense she suspected him to possess, he'd do what it took to get back in his boss's good favor, then return to at least a portion of his former life.

"Now…" When he released her, a part of her wanted to cling to him still. "You look healthy and pretty and like the kind of woman any kid would be happy to call Mom."

His compliment shined a light on a long-buried place within her that had been dark for far too long. But it also made her crave more than just being a good mom. Would she ever have the chance to also be a good wife?

Chapter Twelve

Monday afternoon, while Libby met with Zoe, the gallery owner she'd met at the craft fair, Heath raised his jacket hood against the downpour. Zoe had suggested he return in about an hour, so he ducked into a nearby restaurant for a steaming bowl of chowder.

For a Monday, the place was surprisingly crowded, but he figured the rain had driven tourists from Shore Acres or Cape Arago State Parks into town for something to do.

The next table over held a family of three—parents fussing over a newborn girl who wanted nothing to do with her bottle.

While waiting for his food, Heath alternated his view between the baby and the rivulet-soaked view of the gallery that would hopefully soon house Libby's art.

He'd promised her that if she worked up the courage for this visit, he, in turn, would contact his CO, but as yet, he hadn't found the nerve. It hurt enough missing Patricia while a continent away from where they'd shared their lives. How much worse would it be, blasted by daily reminders like their house, the beach where they'd walked Sam, their friends, her favorite coffee shop or nail salon or the hospice where she'd died? He couldn't bear the vision of the cemetery where she'd been buried.

Once again eyeing the couple with their baby, he struggled with the knowledge that he'd soon be losing Libby, as well—most likely before she even had her baby.

The knowledge shouldn't have bothered him, but did. Just as she had with seemingly every other inhabitant of Bent Road, she'd unwittingly worked her charm on him, as well.

The waitress brought his soup.

The recipe's creamy warmth initially eased his chill, but the more he thought about Libby leaving, him leaving, the more antsy Heath grew. Maybe he wasn't ready to return to his job? There was the matter of Sam to consider. Sure, he could take the dog with him to Virginia Beach, but who would watch him when he was off on a mission? He supposed he could ask Hattie to watch him, or even Pandora—the wife of another one of his team members—but he wouldn't want to impose.

Maybe it was best he stayed put.

In Bent Road, every day was predictable. No highs or lows. Just status quo. At the moment, that suited him just fine.

What about the day you found Libby? What about the night you made love to her in the pool? Weren't those good times?

That hadn't been lovemaking, but sex. Satisfying an itch.

He instantly regretted even thinking such cruel words. She deserved better than a one-night stand.

What do I deserve?

Patricia had wanted him to start a new life without her. He just wasn't sure he could.

What would Patricia think of Libby? Would the two of them have been friends? Heath liked to think so.

The rain had finally let up, but the clouds were still ominous and low.

"Need anything else?" the waitress asked.

"No, thanks. Just the check."

After paying, Heath still had fifteen minutes to kill, so he rounded the block. Thinking, thinking, wondering what was the right thing for him to do.

He'd only burned off five minutes of time and zero nervous energy, so he pulled out his cell and took a deep breath.

His CO answered on the second ring.

"Commander Hewitt, it's Heath Stone. I know last time we spoke, I told you I wouldn't be coming back, but, sir, I've had a change of heart and—"

"Stop right there, son. Are you one hundred percent certain this is what you want? I pulled strings to get you this long of a leave, but I'll move heaven and earth to get you back—if you're sure."

Am I? If he screwed this up, there wouldn't be another chance. On the other hand, if he chose to spend the rest of his life on the course he was on now, he'd not only end up old and alone, but with nothing to show for it. At least if he re-upped, he could be helping people. That sense of once again having purpose was good.

"Stone?" his CO nudged. "Can I count on you to not flake out on me again?"

Heath took a deep breath, then sharply exhaled. "Yes, sir."

"THANK YOU, ZOE," Libby said. "I'll hopefully get at least fifteen or so pieces made before I leave for Seattle. After that, we'll talk."

"Sounds perfect." After a hug, Zoe added, "Let me

know when you have your baby. I want to make sure my new favorite artist and her daughter are healthy and ready to get back to work."

Libby laughed. "Once my mom recovers from the shock of being a surprise grandmother, I'm sure she'll send formal announcements. I'll add you to her list."

She left the gallery, accompanied by the happy tingling of bells on the door.

Outside, the rain had stopped, although the clouds didn't look quite ready to make way for sun. Didn't matter. Libby felt sunny all on her own.

The baby kicked, and she rubbed the spot near her navel. "You're excited, too, huh?"

Libby glanced up to have her afternoon look that much brighter when she found Heath strolling her way. If possible, he seemed taller, his shoulders more broad. His smile took her breath away.

Acting on pure impulse, she ran to him as best she could, crushing him in a hug. "Zoe not only took all five of the pieces I brought her today, but she wants more! I promised her fifteen! Plus, she charges like double what I ever have. Do you have any idea how much money that is? If all of those sell, I'm rich!"

Not thinking, she kissed him with joy.

And then he kissed her back, at first tenderly, but then with an urgency that tempted her to draw him into a private alley to take things to the next level.

"I'm happy for you." He cupped her face with his hands, kissing her again. "You're the first real artist I've met."

"Oh, yeah?" She kissed him.

"Yeah…" As if only just now realizing they stood on the sidewalk of a busy street, making out like horny teens, he shook his head before releasing her and stepping back. "Looks like it's been a big day for both of us."

"What happened for you?" she asked while they walked to his truck.

"I worked up the courage to call my commanding officer."

"And?"

"And…he says he'll take me back." This was huge. Why didn't he look more pleased?

"Heath, that's wonderful! I'm proud of you for taking charge of your life. Why don't you seem more psyched?"

"I am," he said, opening her door, "but he wants me back sooner than I'd expected."

"How soon?"

"Two weeks." Before her baby was due. For some unfathomable reason, the thought sickened her. Odds were her car would be fixed way before then, and once she returned to Seattle, her time with Heath and his mom and uncle would be nothing more than a beautiful memory.

"At least that gives you time for proper goodbyes. What happens with Sam?" When he helped her into the truck there was the usual tangling of arms, but this time with the added pressure of a heady awareness she knew better than to act upon. If she had her way, she'd kiss him again and again, but especially now, she knew for her own emotional well-being she had to keep her hands to herself.

"I want to take him with me, but considering how often I'll be gone, he'll probably be happier with Mom and Fred."

A knot gripped her throat, threatening to close off her oxygen supply. *Don't cry. Don't cry.* "Sounds like a good plan, although I'm sure he'll miss you."

"Not as much as I'll miss him, but your speech back at the beach gave me a much-needed kick in the ass. You were right. About how I'll feel better helping others instead of sitting around my cabin day after day, moping about what might've been."

Don't cry.

"This may sound crazy," he said, bracing himself on her still-open door while rain pattered the windshield, "but the more I'm around you, the more I wonder if instead of me saving you, it was the other way around."

"SO MUCH EXCITEMENT for one day," Gretta said with tears shining in her eyes after Libby and Heath had shared their news. She stepped out from behind the motel's reception desk to deliver double hugs. "I'm so proud of you both. But with you," she said to her son, pinching his cheeks, "I'm also a little miffed. Why didn't you warn me this was your plan?"

Libby felt as though she was intruding upon the intimate mother-and-son scene. A part of her also felt guilty. If it hadn't been for her prodding, would Heath be staying home? Safe and sound in his cabin?

He shrugged and turned away from her to stare out the window. "I wasn't entirely sure myself. After talking with Mason, it just sort of happened. But I'm glad it did. It'll be good for me. I'm restless. I've got to…" When he spun to face her, his eyes had welled. "I've got to move on, you know? Not forget. *Never* forget. But…"

"I understand," Gretta said as she hugged him again. "And I completely, wholeheartedly agree with your decision—at least if you'll let Sam stay with me. I can't bear to think of him being cooped up in a kennel whenever you're gone."

Heath laughed. "Agreed—especially since I was just about to ask if you'd watch him."

As Gretta was wont to do, she turned the night into an impromptu party, inviting not only Mason and Hattie, but Hal and his sons, Eloise and the other women from her poker club and a few of the single fishermen who happened to be staying at the motel.

By nine that night, the scent of steaks on the grill and classic country music filled the cool night air, and Darryl and Terryl played a rowdy game of football in the pool. What little peace the music didn't fill, their rowdy shouts did.

Chilled, seated alone on one of the deck chairs, Libby smiled when Hattie wandered up, offering one of Mason's U.S.Navy sweatshirts. She was happy to take it, but embarrassed that even the men's extra-large strained to cover her belly.

"Thank you," Libby said. "I didn't realize how cold I was."

"You're welcome." Hattie sat next to her. "I always carry layers wherever we go. Seems like ever since I had Charlie, I'm always either super hot or super cold. Never just right."

"Where is the baby?" Libby asked.

"In the rec room, napping in his carrier. Gretta offered to keep an eye on him."

The twins chased Sam, who had as much energy as the munchkins.

Fred, on the other hand, had fallen asleep by the grill.

Hattie said, "You've got to be thrilled about your big art deal, huh?"

Nodding, Libby said, "Zoe even mentioned the possibility that other galleries she's connected with all up and down the West Coast might eventually request to carry my work. It hasn't fully sunk in that I'll soon be able to support myself, but also that I no longer have to constantly travel to art shows to make my living."

"Has this changed where things stand with your folks? Do you think maybe now you might not even go to Seattle?"

Libby shook her head. "I owe it to my daughter to make things right with her grandparents. They're good people. The last thing I want is for her to grow up with no sense of family. I take full responsibility for my part in the events that came between us. I just hope that after all this time they'll accept some responsibility, as well."

"I hope so, too," Hattie said. "And since I'm already being nosy, where do things stand with you and Heath?"

"What do you mean?" Libby's heart lurched. Had he told Mason about their wild night in the pool? And had Mason in turn told his wife?

"How do you feel about him leaving?"

Awful. The more she thought about it, the more depressed she grew. Which made no sense. They barely knew each other. Why couldn't she be happy for him to be getting his life back in order? "I think it's great that he'll be rejoining his friends, doing whatever it is SEALs do."

"Sure—it's great for him, but, Libby, what about you? I've seen the way you two are around each other. Tonight, when you were eating, he hovered, catering to your every need. A guy doesn't do that unless he's trying to impress."

"You're imagining things." Only Libby had noticed, too. And liked the extra attention. In her heart of hearts, she'd even fantasized about a repeat pool performance, but obviously that wasn't meant to be.

"Uh-huh…" Hattie grinned. "How amazing would it be if before Heath leaves, he proposes?"

Libby coughed so hard that Heath jogged over to make sure she wasn't choking. "You all right?"

"Fine." She had been. Then he ran his hand up and down her back, releasing all manner of delicious havoc along her spine.

"Good," he said. "You gave me a scare. Need anything?"

"No, thank you."

"Okay, well, Mason and I are deep into shoptalk, but flag me down if you're thirsty or need a snack."

The second Heath was out of earshot, Hattie asked, "You don't think that was a bit much? I could sit here for a week and it wouldn't occur to Mason to ask me if I need a drink."

Libby thought about Hattie's reflections in regard to Heath for a long time after her new friend was gone. In fact, she couldn't stop thinking about the downright nutty ideas where she and Heath were concerned—especially that bit about him proposing.

Even though the very idea was ludicrous, the one thing Libby couldn't seem to shake was that from the moment the suggestion left Hattie's mouth, Libby realized her answer would be yes.

Not that it mattered, she mused, standing at the rec room's sink, washing serving platters. Even if she and Heath were an item—which they weren't—no way would he be in the market for a second wife. Not when he'd already had perfection.

But because she had nothing better to dwell on while

scrubbing a deviled egg plate, what would it hurt to indulge in a daydream at this time of night?

Heath would be everything Liam hadn't been. Dependable. Loyal. Take-her-breath-away sexy. Judging from the times she'd watched him play with Vivian and Vanessa, he'd also be great with kids. She sighed.

"Give you a buck-fifty for your thoughts?" He'd snuck up beside her, causing her to jump.

"That's an awful lot of cash, big spender." She grinned in his direction, willing her pulse to slow when he grinned right back.

"What can I say? The way your forehead was so adorably scrunched in concentration, I figured I'd for sure get my money's worth."

No kidding! "Sad for you—" she crossed her fingers beneath the suds for the fib she was about to tell "—that the only thing on my mind is wondering how to best tackle the baked bean pan."

"How about you sit—like you're supposed to be doing—and let me scrub it?"

"That'll work." She wiped her hands on a dish towel, then backed into the nearest chair, content to let her gaze wander to his strong shoulders and biceps and the way he did an excellent job of filling out the backside of his faded jeans.

After cleaning the cast-iron skillet that had held the beans, he asked, "What're your plans for tomorrow?"

"I almost forgot. It's the Fourth, isn't it?"

"Yes, ma'am. There's a parade and the carnival we still haven't been to. The barbecue cook-off in the park, and then fireworks at the beach."

"I'm exhausted just hearing about all of it. Got anything more low-key? Assuming you were asking me to tag along with you to any of those events?"

"I was asking, and what do you think of fishing? I know of a nice, shady spot by the river that I can pull the truck right up to." He finished washing a baking sheet. "If we have any luck, I'll catch you a couple fat trout, then fry them for you for dinner. Sound good?"

Unable to speak past yet another knot of happiness in her throat, she nodded.

"You okay?" he asked while drying his hands on the same towel she'd used.

"I'm great."

"Then what's with the waterworks?"

"I'm not sure…" Only she was. Honestly, her latest round of tears were because never in her life had she shared a more intense chemistry with a man. Heath held the power to infuriate her one minute, then have her laughing the next. He was sexy-hot, but also tender and kind. If she hadn't been carrying another man's baby, and if he hadn't been headed to relaunch his career in Virginia Beach, who knew what the two of them might've shared?

Chapter Thirteen

"Don't yell at me!" Libby said above the river's gurgling rush when she'd fouled up his fly rod yet again. Heath had promised this stretch of river would be gentle, but he'd failed to account for the previous day's deluge.

"I'm not yelling. But, Lib, you're not even trying to do it right. Plus, we really should be out by that deeper pool, but in your condition, I'm not sure that's such a great idea."

"You think?" she snapped. Had it been only last night when she'd thought he'd make good relationship material?

"Okay, let's try this again." Making her all the more flustered, he stood behind her, easing his arms around her, covering her hands in what she assumed was an attempt to demonstrate the proper way to hold a rod. Alas, all it really achieved was making her entire backside tingle.

"What I need you to do is hold the pole parallel to the water."

What I need you to do is kiss the spot on my neck where your warm breath is making me all achy.

"Next, keeping your elbows by your sides, you'll need to draw the pole back to about the two o'clock position."

Or, we could just stop pretending I'll ever catch on to this technique and spend the rest of the afternoon making out on that picnic blanket you stashed in the truck bed.

"Once the line's straight, snap it back to ten o'clock."

Oh—she could snap something, all right. Maybe his boxers' elastic waistband?

"See how the line's straightening out? Now, you want to guide the fly, presenting it like a gift to our waiting fish...."

She licked her lips. Oh, my, what she'd love to gift him with...

"Make sense?"

"I'm sorry, what?" Was it possible to actually be dizzy from desire? Did he have any idea how good he smelled? Like a leathery, sweat-salty blend that encompassed her every male fantasy?

"Libby? Haven't you heard a word I've said?"

"Yes, but—" *my rich fantasy world is* way *more entertaining* "—maybe I'm not cut out to be a fisherwoman?"

"But we drove all the way out here to fish."

"What if I watch you fish?"

"Isn't that going to be boring for you?"

Have you looked in a mirror lately? "Probably, but I've got Sam and a good book to keep me company. Or maybe I'll take a nap?" She feigned a yawn.

"Want me to drive you back to Mom's?"

"Not at all." What she really wanted was a kiss, but since that wasn't likely to happen, she'd settle for watching him from afar. "Go ahead, catch me a big, fat fish. Then we'll talk."

He blanched. "Why does that sound ominous?"

"It shouldn't. Relax and enjoy yourself. Before too long, this will all be a memory."

HEATH KNEW LIBBY had meant her words to be comforting, but she couldn't have done a better job of missing that mark. Her not-so-subtle reminder that in a short time he'd not only be leaving this wild place that he loved, with its sun rays slanting through fragrant pines and boulders strewn along the river's edge like a giant's game of marbles, but he'd also be leaving her.

How had she come to mean so much in so little time? He hardly knew anything about her, yet he craved knowing everything.

Even worse than the guilt stemming from wanting his next taste of her was the curiosity he held for her unborn child. What would the baby look like? Would she have her mother's blue eyes and curls? Freckles? Cute giggle?

He found himself fighting an irrational longing to share those precious first days with mother and child, but then what? What would he even have to offer a woman so—literally and figuratively—full of life as Libby? Where his emotions were concerned, he'd long since established himself to be an empty shell.

Still… In between casts, he glanced in her direction. She sat on the blanket she'd spread beneath a towering fir. While she read a tattered paperback from his mother's library, Sam happily snoozed with his head on her thighs. Every so often, she stroked the soft fur behind his dog's ears. Heath knew the texture well, as it was his favorite place to give Sam affection.

Just looking at her produced a foreign tightening in his chest. A yearning for the kind of closeness he'd once shared with Patricia, but would never be his again.

Why?

The lone word resonated deep within him. It suddenly turned his carefully constructed emotional walls to dust.

His whole reason for keeping Libby at a safe distance was because of his promise to Patricia. But with her blessing for him to forge ahead with a new life, new meaning, what held him back?

His loyalty for her? Yes.

His rock solid belief in the sanctity of their marriage? Hell, yes.

But through no fault of their own, death had seen fit to part them far sooner than either had expected. So where did that leave him? Was he wrong to crave not only more of Libby's kisses, but the comfort and solace he found when he held her in his arms? In the pool, inside her, he'd felt alive and empowered and as if Libby had been the gatekeeper holding the key to this new dawn of his life.

All of a sudden Heath found himself jealous of his dog and the attention Libby lavished upon him.

Though he hadn't caught a single fish he'd promised Libby for dinner, he removed his hip waders, tossed the rest of his gear in the back of the truck, then joined her on the blanket.

"Already catch your limit?"

He laughed. "Try none."

"What're you planning to feed me? As usual, my back hurts and I'm starving, and your mother's spoiled me rotten when it comes to eating a lot—often."

"I know. Sorry. Some days they just aren't biting." Or, more likely in his case, he'd been so distracted by her beauty that he couldn't have caught a trout if it jumped in his back pocket.

"Uh-huh…" Her grin did funny things to his stomach. "Likely story. So what are you going to feed me? Besides another line about the fish not biting."

"How about we go to a little town south of here? We'll

buy salmon from this guy who smokes them fresh from the boats. Then, we'll drive up to Calabash Point, and watch the firework shows all the way from Bent Road to Marble Falls?"

The light behind her eyes was all the answer he needed. But it didn't hurt his ego when she said, "Not only do I love smoked salmon, but when you smile at me like that, I'd go pretty much anywhere with you."

"LET ME HOLD your hand. Sometimes, the dock can be slick."

"Sure," Libby said, easing her fingers between Heath's. Though his explanation for his actions was plausible, it lost credence considering the sun-faded wood planks were dry.

As they strolled past commercial fishing boats and mom-and-pop charters, Libby couldn't shake the sensation of fleeting perfection. Perfection in the sense that never had she felt more at ease or content. Fleeting with the knowledge that in two weeks—sooner if her car was repaired—this lovely dream of being with Heath would end.

The pale blue sky was streaked with early evening oranges, reds and violets, and the temperature by the water was cooler than it had been in the lot where they'd parked the truck.

When she shivered, Heath bought her an oversize Oregon hoodie from a tourist shop.

Outside of the shop, he paused to help tug it over her curls. When it got stuck, he pulled it the rest of the way down, landing him once again in perfect kissing range.

This time, instead of kissing him, Libby's pride forced her to wait for him to close the distance. Lucky for her, the wait wasn't long.

"You're beautiful," he whispered so softly she wasn't sure she'd heard it at all.

His kiss managed to all at once be sweet and tender and laced with the urgency stemming from knowing their time together would be brief. If this was indeed the start of a relationship, sadly, the end was already in sight.

"Get a room!" a passing teen hollered from his bike.

Laughing, Libby regrettably called a halt to the impromptu make-out session. "Do you always have dessert before dinner?"

"Hell, yeah…" Though his language was all man, Heath's expression came closer to one worn by a boy caught eating the ice cream straight from the carton. "Don't you think it's better that way?"

She kissed him again. "Yes. Definitely."

They resumed their gentle stroll to the smoked fish stand, sharing more laughs and kisses at the picnic table where they ate their meal.

From there, they took their time returning to the truck.

As much as Libby cherished their every moment together, the day's activities had worn her out to the extent that she napped all the way to the lookout point.

"Wake up, sleepyhead."

"Mmm…" She slowly stirred, pleased to find Heath's smiling face once again within kissing range. "Are we there?"

"Yes. But unfortunately, I'm not as original as I thought, because there are about a dozen families up here with the same bright idea."

"That's okay," she said, gazing over the glistening Pacific. The sun had set, but the moon was now rising, fat and happy as if enjoying the holiday as much as the rest of the crowd. "This will be even more fun. I love hearing everyone ooh and ahh for the really fancy ones."

He helped her from the truck, then took the picnic blanket from the back, spreading it on a grassy area amongst the rest of the parents and kids and grandparents and young lovers.

What had Heath been like before his heart had been shattered and his hopes disillusioned?

"Did you used to come here as a kid?" she asked once they got settled. She sat between his legs, leaning against his chest for support. Her hands rested atop the baby and Heath's hands were atop hers. His heat warmed her, protecting her from the chilly night air.

"Once in a while. Mostly—if my dad was lucky enough to be on leave for the holiday, and was stationed close enough that we could visit my grandparents—they took us to the beach in Bent Road. I'd set up a lounge chair in the sand, pretending I was a tough guy while drinking root beer and smoking candy cigarettes."

"My, my," she teased, "weren't you the rebel."

He laughed. "All right, Miss Jailbird, what are some of your favorite Independence Day memories?"

Libby turned introspective. She preferred not to think of her parents at all, but back when she'd been a kid and hadn't yet learned there was a way of life that didn't involve wearing heels and pearls for every occasion, she supposed she'd had at least a little fun. "First, I'm not proud of my time behind bars. I was in the wrong."

"Sorry. I was poking fun where I shouldn't have."

"You're forgiven."

"Whew…" He feigned relief by sweeping back her hair to kiss the bit of her neck he'd bared. His warm kiss in the cool night air brought on shivers so delicious she temporarily forgot her aching lower back.

"Cold?"

She shook her head, snuggling closer.

"Good. So back to your story?"

"Mom and I always wore matching custom dresses, of course, in red, white and blue. Or some variation thereof. Dad's tie matched, too. Some years we watched fireworks on yachts. Other years, from the house."

"And by 'house,' you mean freakishly ostentatious mansion?"

She cringed. "I suppose you could call it that. But I just called it home, at least until I hit my rebellious years. The cook, maids, gardeners and chauffeurs were as much—or more—parents to me as Mom and Dad. Looking back on it, I suppose they did the best they could in raising me, but my grandparents on both sides were just like them, so they were probably mimicking their own upbringings. Anyway, at my house, a picnic consisted of the servants setting up an elaborate outdoor sit-down meal. Children were rarely invited to sit with the adults, and when we were, we were expected to be seen and not heard."

"So were you friends with the other rich kids?"

"Some of them. But in high school I volunteered because my guidance counselor said it looked good on college applications. I don't think anyone expected me to actually enjoy it. I met all kinds of new people. Once I realized how different I was from the rest of the world, and just how much of a difference I could make to the local homeless shelter by donating my monthly clothing allowance, something inside me changed. Though lately I've been too busy eking out a living to do as much charity work as I used to, one of these days I'd like to get back to volunteering."

"That's cool. If this gallery thing with Zoe works out, you might have more time. You know, spend a few days a week on your art, then the rest of your time working at a shelter or some other place where you'd feel needed."

"I like that plan." Almost as much as she liked him.

The fireworks began.

Even though Heath explained they were ten miles from either town, from this high, on a night so clear, both displays could be seen in Technicolor glory—even faint booms could every so often be heard.

More than the actual show, Libby enjoyed the camaraderie that came along with sharing the occasion with so many appreciative folks. The oohs and ahs and hearty applause by far outshone any of the brightest displays.

Eyes closed against stinging tears, she swallowed hard, recalling a long-ago summer night....

Libertina, you mustn't jump or cry out during the fireworks display. Never forget that above all, you're a lady. Daddy and I expect you to behave as such.

Hugging her baby, Libby decided she'd encourage her daughter to behave with zero decorum. In fact, the very word would be shunned in her home.

When the shows from both towns had finished with spectacular grand finales, Libby was so tired she needed Heath's help to stand.

It was strange to think that only a short time ago, she'd been embarrassed about needing his assistance. Now she welcomed his every touch.

"Have fun?" he asked, setting a slow pace for the return to the truck.

"This was my best Fourth of July ever. Thank you so much."

"You're welcome. Judging by where we both are this

time next year, maybe we could do it again—only next time with your daughter along for the ride."

"I'd like that," she said, even though the possibility of them ever meeting again once they went their separate ways was slim.

The notion made her unspeakably sad.

HEATH WOKE TO a renewed sense of purpose.

He and Sam did a ten-mile run. It felt strange wearing his boots again, but they'd slipped on like a pair of good friends. They'd seen a lot of action together and it was a rush to think they soon would again.

Mason and Hattie would be leaving today for a brief stay in Alaska to visit their respective parents. Mason's mom had died when he'd been a child, but as far as Heath knew, both of Hattie's parents were still alive, and eager to see their grandkids.

Up until the past couple days with Libby, Heath had been looking forward to getting back to the privacy of his cabin, but now that his time in Bent Road was limited, he'd have just as soon camped out on his mom's sofa. He wished he could tell himself it was her motherly love he craved, but he wouldn't have been fooling anyone.

Libby's blue eyes, easy smile and gorgeous hair had him hooked far more effectively than the trout he'd tried catching. Trouble was, he wasn't trying to catch her. If anything—given the fact that the clock was ticking on the time he had left in town—he should give her a wide berth.

On the deserted beach playground, he did eight pull-ups on the monkey bars before he was shaking from the exertion. Not acceptable, considering he'd need fifteen to twenty to be competitive. Ten was the minimum. Sit-ups and push-ups weren't his idea of a good time, but they were at least doable at a hundred each. As for how long it had taken him to complete the exercises? No comment.

Despite the morning fog and brisk temperature, he'd worked up a hellacious sweat. Knowing he also needed serious boning up on his swimming skills, he stripped down to his skivvies and dove into the surf. The water was cold—like dunking in a vat of ice—but now was hardly the time to wimp out. He only had a short while to get in some semblance of shape, and although he knew there was no way he'd be where he wanted by the time he reported for duty, for his own pride, he'd have to be a helluva lot further along than he was now.

Finished with what he gauged to be three-hundred yards—two-hundred shy of his minimum—Heath sloshed his way out of the water and collapsed on the sand.

Even Sam was exhausted, crashing alongside him, panting.

Heath rolled over to his gear to grab his water bottle, then poured some into his hand for the dog to lap. After repeating this drill three times, Sam fell back asleep and Heath drank some for himself.

He was mortified to have let himself go to this degree. Instead of fishing every day, why hadn't he at least had enough personal pride to maintain his physical strength?

The answer was a no-brainer. Grief did funny things to a man. It made him doubt everything he'd once cherished. Losing Patricia had been the equivalent of having his life's foundation ripped out from under him. Without her, he'd been lost.

Now he felt better, but ironically, it had taken another woman to get him there. As much as he'd grown to care for Libby, he didn't like the fact that he hadn't been able to reach inside himself for self-motivation. What had Libby given him that he hadn't been able to find on his own?

Another easy answer—even when he had believed himself incapable of anything more than the most rudimentary motions of getting through his days, she'd believed him capable of so much more. Her strength had become his. And he'd always be grateful. But what else would she expect from him? What else did she deserve? What was he even capable of giving?

Last night had been the best he'd had in years.

Death had been an insidious, cumbersome beast that had starved him and Patricia of happiness and dignity and quality time.

Watching those fireworks, holding Libby in his arms, he'd felt ridiculously high—and capable of anything. But this morning, faced with his lackluster physical performance, he knew the rest of his time in Bent Road needed to not be spent holding hands or making out, but working himself to the edge of his physical endurance, then pushing still harder.

As for where Libby fit in that picture?

As much as it pained him to admit, she didn't.

Chapter Fourteen

Libby woke to hard rain pelting her bedroom window, but even a glum day couldn't dampen her mood.

Her night with Heath had been romantic beyond anything she'd ever imagined. Sure, there may not have been candles or roses or fine chocolate, but she was a low-maintenance gal, and smoked salmon and holding hands and fireworks had made for a perfect first date.

After a yawn and stretch, Libby gasped from sharper than usual lower back pain. She'd had Braxton Hicks contractions, but this was different—more of a sharp pain. She was so huge, she had to roll from the bed.

Once up, she stopped off at the bathroom. After taking care of necessities, she fluffed her hair, brushed her teeth and pressed a cool washcloth to her splotchy face. It'd been so long since she'd seen her real figure, she'd forgotten what she looked like.

Would Heath have been attracted to her back when she wore a size six, or was her baby part of what drew him to her? She knew he'd wanted to be a dad.... Could part of him wonder what it might be like to become part of a ready-made family? Was that why he was with her?

But then was he truly *with* her at all? Both of them

would soon go their separate ways, meaning this was little more than a fling to him.

The notion made her sad. But realistically, it also forced her to search her own motives. What did she hope to gain from their last few days together? More making out? More skinny-dipping? More of the simple, basic comfort that stemmed from talking with a friend?

Sighing, she knew she'd never figure it all out in the next few seconds, so she got on with her day, ignoring the especially nagging ache in her lower back in favor of maybe nabbing a secret, good-morning kiss.

Only she didn't find Heath on the couch, but Fred, gnawing on a slimy rawhide she knew he wasn't allowed to have on the furniture.

He froze, as if in hopes that if he didn't move she wouldn't see him, and as soon as she left he could carry on. When that technique didn't work, he applied a guilty tilt to his head and wide-eyed innocence.

"You're not fooling me," she said, pointing toward his perfectly comfy bed. "Down."

He begrudgingly obeyed.

She soon found that she and Fred were on their own. Hattie and Mason were heading to the airport, so was Heath at the cabin? But that didn't make sense, because Hattie had promised to stop by to say goodbye.

Though her aching back made every step agony, Libby waddled to the motel office in search of Gretta.

"Good morning, sleepyhead." Heath's mom looked up from a stack of bills and her checkbook. "What time did you two get in last night?"

Libby yawned. "I think it was around midnight. After dinner, Heath drove me to watch the fireworks from a point—I can't remember the name."

"Calabash?"

"That's it. We had so much fun." Libby left out the part where she and Heath had lingered long after the rest of the crowd had left. They had shared kisses and conversation. He'd shared his thoughts and fears on returning to the navy and she, in turn, had voiced her concerns about single-parenthood and failing to reconnect with her family.

"I can tell. You're glowing."

Hands to her cheeks, Libby said, "I'm sure I'm just hot from the walk over."

"Nope." Gretta smiled. "Don't even try fooling me. I didn't just fall off the turnip truck. I know sparks of romance when I see them. My son's finally courting you, and I couldn't be more pleased." She rounded the desk to give Libby a hug. Only instead of returning her friend's embrace, Libby winced.

"What's wrong?" Gretta asked, her expression pinched with concern. "Something to do with the baby?"

"No…" Libby backed onto one of the lobby's comfy leather chairs. "I think I spent too much of yesterday sitting on the ground. Too little support left me using muscles my body apparently forgot I had."

Gretta didn't seem so sure. "Let me know if you feel worse. You could be in back labor."

"Thanks for worrying, but I'm fine."

AN HOUR LATER, Libby wasn't so sure. If anything, her back pain was even more intense. Still, with Hattie and Mason at the house with the kids, she didn't want to waste a moment of their goodbyes worrying about a minor ache.

"I'm going to miss you," Libby said to her new friend, rocking her in a hug.

"Likewise," Hattie said, along with a kiss to Libby's cheek. "I was selfishly hoping for a super sneaky surprise engagement so I could have you with me at home. We SEAL wives are always looking to recruit quality ladies for our single guys, as opposed to the female flotsam that sometimes washes up in my bar."

Libby laughed. "Sorry, but there's no chance of a proposal from Heath—or even a kiss—in my future."

"Uh-huh… Deny it all you want, but you can't fool me. I know you two have something going on."

Libby couldn't help but grin through her latest wince. "What's it going to take for you to believe me?"

"Hmm…" She tapped her upper lip with her index finger. "How about a marriage license to another guy?"

"Now you're talking crazy." Because Libby couldn't imagine herself with anyone other than Heath. A definite problem since this morning, after returning from his workout, he'd been uncharacteristically cold, reminding her of the way things had been between them when she'd first come to town. Which, in light of the good times they'd recently shared, made no sense. A fact she planned to drill him on the moment Hattie and Mason hit the road. "But in the unlikely event I do get married, you'll be the first to know."

"Thank you."

"Hat Trick." Mason tugged the back of his wife's lightweight jacket. "If we're going to make our flight, we've got to go."

"Okay, okay…" Libby's throat tightened when Hattie gave her one more hug. "Don't rush me."

"Babe, it's not me putting a time limit on you, but the airline."

Being overly emotional wasn't new territory for Libby, but she was surprised by just how much she hated seeing Hattie go. Sure, she could talk to Gretta, but having a woman her own age to talk to had been a lot of fun.

"Bye, Wibby!" Vivian and Vanessa ambushed Libby's legs with sweet hugs.

"Aw, goodbye, you two. It was so nice meeting you. Hope I see you again real soon."

"Uh-huh," Vivian said.

Vanessa busied herself kissing Sam.

"All right," Mason said, "Libby, it was a pleasure meeting you, but we've really got to go. Come on, crew…" As Mason herded his brood out the door and to their rented SUV, Libby felt a profound sense of loss.

She now knew the friends she thought she'd had on her craft show circuit hadn't been true. What kind of friend carried on business as usual while knowing the man Libby loved was engaging in multiple affairs?

As if sensing Libby's sadness, Gretta wrapped her arm around her shoulders. "It's okay. Now that you and Heath are an item, I'm sure you'll see all of them again soon."

"But we're not—"

"Hush. It's disrespectful to lie to your elders."

"What about you and Hal?" Libby asked, glad Heath was still talking to Mason. "I've seen you two together. When are you going to make an official declaration?"

Blushing furiously, Gretta waved off Libby's question. "Stop being fresh and get out of here. You should be resting."

Mmm…a nap did sound divine—if only she fell asleep cocooned by Heath's strong arms. Too bad that sort of pleasure would only be found in her dreams.

HEATH HAD MIXED feelings watching his friends go. He knew once he returned to Virginia Beach, once he rejoined the old crew, he'd be with them probably more than he'd like, so what bugged him about their leaving?

His answer was found when he looked Libby's way to find his mother consoling her.

What bugged him was the fact that today marked the first of many tough goodbyes. His mom and Uncle Morris traditionally visited often, but he wouldn't soon see his dog, and Libby... How did he even start letting her go? Especially when she wasn't even his?

Gretta cleared her throat. "Well, you two. I need to get back to washing towels. Libby, do you need anything before I go?"

"No, thank you."

On her own with Heath, Libby wasn't sure what to say, so she settled for chitchat. "How was your workout?"

"Good." He aimed for the house.

"What's wrong?" Following him, still holding her throbbing back, she said, "You seem like a different person from the guy I was with last night."

"You're imagining things." He held open the back door for her.

Sam romped past them both, knocking her into Heath. He easily supported her, saving her from toppling, but the moment he had her safely upright he let her go. There was none of the lingering contact she'd grown to expect—and enjoy. Instead, he'd become a study in cold efficiency.

"Am I? Last night you couldn't keep your hands off of me. Now you act as if I have cholera."

"Point of fact—" he took a bottled water from the fridge "—the odds of catching cholera from person to person isn't all that high, but you damn sure wanna watch where you get your water."

"Thanks, Mr. Walking Encyclopedia."

He finished half the bottle in one gulp. "Just sayin'…"

"W-what's wrong with you?" Her lower back screamed, but her questioning heart hurt worse. "Last night you were funny and romantic and considerate. Now?" She shook her head. "You're being an ass. I don't even know you."

"Ever think you shouldn't?"

"What's that mean?"

Ignoring her, he left for the living room and started cramming his clothes and books and Sam's toys into a duffel. From there, he headed for the bathroom, shoveling in his toiletries, as well.

"Answer me." She tried tugging him around by his shirtsleeve, but he stood firm. The effort cost her dearly, as the stretch left her doubling over in pain. *"Ouch…"*

As if her need had flipped a hidden switch deep within him, tender, caring Heath was back, ushering her to a chair. "What's wrong? Is it your back?"

She nodded, but the pain had grown to such an extent that she lacked the focus to speak.

"Shit…" Tossing his duffel, he scooped her into his arms, stormed through the house to kick open the back door, then somehow got her into the truck. Without slowing to even tell his mom where they were going, he drove straight to the clinic, stopping in front of the stairs.

"Stay put," he barked. "I'm gonna get help."

She did as he asked, hugging her baby, crying and moaning for relief. What was wrong with her? Was her baby okay? This kind of pain couldn't be normal.

Moments later, Heath returned with Doc Meadows, Lacy and Eloise in tow.

After Heath hefted Libby from the truck to a wheelchair, the doctor took over, pushing her up the ramp and into an exam room. She wanted Heath with her, holding her hand, reassuring her everything would be all right, but he wasn't following and she was too consumed with pain to ask.

HEATH HAD BEEN in the clinic's waiting room listening to Libby's muted cries for fifteen minutes before he couldn't take a second more.

Ignoring a coughing kid and his mom, Heath stormed past Eloise to the closed door leading to the exam rooms.

"You can't go back there!" Eloise shouted, chasing after him while he searched room by room until finding poor Libby.

"Babe…" he said, surprised to find her on her hands and knees on a blanket stretched across the floor. "Why aren't you on the examination table?" To the doctor he barked, "What's up with her being down there? Can't you see she's in pain?"

Doc Meadows sat on a rolling stool, scribbling something on Libby's chart before even looking up. "Relax, son. This might look odd, but I can assure you I've delivered hundreds of healthy kiddos and I've got this under control. The baby's heartbeat is strong, but Libby's baby's in what's called an occiput posterior position. In layman's terms, the hardest part of the baby's skull is resting on Libby's spine. What we're going to do is try coaxing the baby into a more favorable position. In the meantime, I want Libby like this to take the pressure off of her back."

"How long does she have to stay like that?"

"Unfortunately, as long as it takes. The good news is that she's already at six centimeters, so she's well on her way to a safe delivery, I just want to apply pressure to convince this little one to turn around."

Heath's head was spinning. In a situation like this, he

wanted to call on his training to get Libby safely through this crisis, but how could he do that when he obviously knew nothing about labor or delivery?

"What can I do to help?" he asked.

"Honestly," Doc Meadows said, "I'd feel a lot better with you back out in the waiting room."

That might be what the doctor wanted, but what did Libby want? "Lib?" he asked, sickened by the pain marring her beautiful features. Her lips formed a tight grimace and her eyes were shut. Every few seconds, she moaned. Sweat dampened her forehead, and the nurse had already pulled Libby's long hair into a ponytail. "Do you want me to stay? I will—if you need me."

As if she were in a trance, she didn't even look his way. Had she heard him? Did he need to get on her level to make sure?

"Heath," Doc Meadows repeated, "you need to go. I know it may not seem like it to you, but all of this is natural. Libby and her baby will be fine. If I spot even the smallest sign of mother or child being in distress, I can have her transported to a hospital in thirty minutes."

"Shouldn't she just go now?"

"It'll only increase her discomfort."

"Still…"

The doctor pointed him toward the door.

Chapter Fifteen

"Honey, you need to relax," Heath's mother said three hours into Libby's ordeal. While he paced the clinic's waiting room, with Eloise glaring in his direction, she added, "She's in good hands. Doc Meadows has delivered ninety percent of the kids born in this county. I know that look on your face. You're thinking this is going to end badly, like Patricia, but sweetheart, having a baby hurts. That's just how it is. But in the end, when you hold that precious bundle in your arms, the pain magically vanishes and all that's left is love."

"Yeah, but why won't the doctor let me back there? Shouldn't someone she knows be with her? At least holding her hand? I've seen how this goes on TV and movies, and the dad's always in there with the mom. You know, like a family."

"But, sweetie, you're not a family. As much as she's come to mean to me—and I suspect, to you—when you get right to it, we hardly know her at all."

But that wasn't how he wanted it to be.

Why had he been such an ass this morning? Determined to push her away when all he really wanted was for them to be closer? But it wasn't right for him to welcome her into his life just as he was leaving—her, too, for that matter. He'd been about to explain that to her before bringing her here.

"Do you care for her?" Gretta asked under her breath, presumably so only he could hear.

"Of course," he snapped. "Why else would I be a nervous wreck?"

"No." She rose to rub his back. "I mean do you really care for her? As in have feelings beyond friendship?"

What could he say? Of course, he did. But he shouldn't. And the guilt was eating him alive. It was no longer about guilt over Patricia, but the fact that he was in no shape to emotionally support anyone. Hell, these past months he'd barely cared for Sam. Libby and her baby deserved way more than he had to offer.

"I know you do," his mom said, "so you can stop with the act of playing it cool."

He drew her into the area of the clinic that had once been the grand home's foyer. "Okay, so what if I do have feelings for her? That doesn't change anything. I'm leaving. She's leaving. It would never work between us."

"Why?" Her crossed arms and jutted chin told him she fully meant her question. "Come on, Heath, I dare you to give me one legitimate reason why two lovely young people who clearly need each other should spend even one day apart. And these days, distance doesn't count. It's not as if she'd have to take a covered wagon east to be with you."

"You're not funny." He pressed his fingertips to his stinging eyes.

"I'm not trying to be."

"Heath?" The nurse appeared. "The doctor has the baby turned, and Libby's ready to push. She asked for you."

"TH-THANK YOU, FOR BEING HERE," Libby managed, out of her mind with pain and looking for any comfort. Right now, the only thing she could think of to bring her a moment's peace was Heath.

"Of course, angel. Where else would I be?" He stood at the head of the bed in one of the two hospital-type rooms the doctor used for any patients he needed to keep a closer eye on, but who weren't sick enough to be transported to Coos Bay.

"Enough chitchat," the doctor said. "Libby, girl, I'm gonna need you to push for all your worth."

Teeth clenched, Libby held tight to Heath, craving not only his comfort, but strength.

She had no idea how long she'd been pushing, but forever didn't seem too terribly out of line. Day had turned to night, and through it all he'd stood alongside her, pressing cool rags to her forehead and sweeping back her hair. Telling her she was beautiful, and he couldn't wait to meet her baby girl, who would no doubt be as pretty as her.

Over and over, she bore down. And every time, just when she thought she couldn't stand any more pain, Heath gave her hand a reassuring squeeze.

"She's crowning!" the doctor finally said. "Come on, Libby. You're almost there."

"Arrrrgggghhh!" she cried. "I can't!"

"Yes, you can," Heath assured.

"Nooooooo…" She thrashed her head back and forth, gritting her teeth through agonizing pain.

"Come on, angel," Heath coached. "Stay strong just a little longer and you'll be holding your gorgeous baby in your arms. One more push."

"E-easy for you to say…"

He laughed. "That's my girl. Get mad at me if it helps. I deserve it."

"Y-yes, you do…"

"What did I tell you two about the chatter," the doctor said. "Libby, I need you to focus like you never have before. One or two more pushes and you'll be done."

She nodded, bearing down, squeezing Heath's hand for all she was worth. *"Arrrggghh…"*

All at once came tremendous pressure, then bliss when pain was replaced by her baby's precious first cry.

And then, when the doctor placed her daughter on her chest, Libby was crying and laughing, as was Heath.

"She's amazing," he said, his voice an awestruck whisper. "I've never seen anything more perfect."

"Hello," Libby said to her daughter, skimming her hand over her tiny fingers and toes. "Boy, am I glad to see you."

Everyone present laughed.

After more bonding, the doctor asked Heath to step out.

Once the infant's cord was cut, the doctor volunteered to clean up the baby while the nurse helped Libby.

"By this time tomorrow," the nurse said, "you'll be surprised by how much better you'll feel."

"Hope so," Libby said with a faint smile.

Twenty minutes later, the efficient nurse had cleaned Libby, dressed her in a new patient gown and tidied the room. Anyone who hadn't been present during nearly the entire day of labor would have never guessed what had just happened.

"I'm sure Gretta and Eloise are itching to see you and the baby. Feel up to a short visit?"

Since Gretta was the only mother figure currently in her life, Libby nodded.

HEATH HOVERED OVER Doc Meadows, who, in turn, hovered over Libby's baby girl.

He considered himself blessed to have witnessed quite a few things in his life, but watching this perfect, tiny creature enter the world had been better than watching the sunrise from atop Kilimanjaro.

"Good job," the doctor said upon filling out a sheet with Apgar Score Table in bold letters at the top.

"What's that?" Heath asked.

With a chuckle, Doc Meadows said, "This little lady's first standardized test. It scores her color, muscle tone, activity level and so on."

"How's she doing?"

"Solid eight out of ten. She's a smidge early, so at six pounds, she's smaller than I'd like, but other than that I see no cause for alarm."

Heath released the breath he'd been holding.

"You were great with Libby. I'm sure she appreciated your help."

"Thanks, but I didn't do much."

"Don't be so sure. Labor's one of the scariest things a woman can go through. The fact that you held strong for Libby I'm sure means the world to her. Gives the two of you a nice, solid foundation for your shared future."

"Whoa, whoa, whoa…" Heath held up his hands. "You know I'm not the father, right?"

"Sure, but what would it hurt if you were? Libby's going to need a lot of help in the coming days and months. I can't think of a better man to tackle the job."

Heath wasn't so sure, but it somehow meant a lot to him that the doctor who'd known him since he was a kid held him in such high regard. Heath wished he deserved the praise—especially after the way he'd treated

Libby this morning. Just because he was messed up inside didn't mean he had to take her along for the ride.

After swaddling the sleeping infant in a thick cotton blanket, Doc Meadows handed her to Heath. "Want the honors of being the first to show her off to her mom and the woman who will hopefully soon be her grandmother?"

Of course, Heath took the baby, but again felt the doctor was getting way ahead of himself.

Then he looked down just as the still nameless baby girl opened blue eyes that reminded him so much of Libby's. Sure, he'd heard the old adage that all babies have blue eyes, but not like this. She was breathtaking all the way from her few pale blond whisps of curls to her tiny, perfect fingernails.

A knot formed at the back of his throat that refused to let go. He made it through the next thirty minutes in slow motion, almost as if he were underwater. While his mom and Eloise and the nurse cooed over the baby, he resumed his place at the head of the bed, beside Libby, stroking her hair, bringing her water, making sure the new mom was as comfortable as possible.

Once Gretta and the other women left, Heath watched as Libby first tried her hand at breastfeeding, his heart impossibly full. He had a feeling the image of her with her daughter at her breast would stay with him a long time—if not forever.

"What're you going to name her?" he asked.

"Gosh, I suppose with all the excitement around my car and meeting all of you in Bent Road, I haven't even thought about it. I figured I still had a couple weeks to figure it out, you know?"

He nodded. "Well, I suppose Heathette's out of the picture, but I think it has a nice ring."

"You're incorrigible," she said with a faint grin.

"I—I want—need—to apologize for the way I treated you this morning. After working out, and realizing just how out of shape I am…" He ran his fingers along the bed's cool metal rail. "Well, I figured if I just made a clean break from you then focused on my training, I'd be all right, you know?"

Eyes welling, she nodded.

"But after what we shared, I see it's not that simple. I'm not sure when it happened, but you've come to mean a lot to me. And I need you to know that I'm not pulling that freeze-out crap again, okay? You deserve better."

"Thank you."

Though he nodded, he didn't feel worthy of her thanks.

"What would you say if I called the baby Heather?"

His heart nearly burst. "I'd say you're probably nuts, but hey, who am I to complain?"

A WEEK LATER, Libby had settled into somewhat of a routine with Baby Heather. She'd found that the only truly dependable part of motherhood was the fact that if she wasn't breastfeeding, she was changing diapers, or rocking, or singing lullabies. Oh—and just staring in wonder at the miracle of her baby girl.

"Ninety-nine, one hundred…"

From her cozy perch on Gretta's backyard swing, Libby paused the stopwatch Heath had given her to monitor his training.

Heather stirred from her slight movement, but didn't wake.

"How was it?" he asked, still breathing hard.

"You're under four minutes, but if you're serious about making it to two minutes, you've got a ways to go."

He groaned, collapsing onto the grass.

"You'll get there. And you shaved a whole minute off your run this morning." Libby loved that instead of excluding her from his workout routine, he let her help. The sensation of them working toward a common goal only made her feel that much closer to him.

"I know, but I want to be at the top of my game when I get back on base."

"Obviously, but even you said you can already notice a difference in how much better you're feeling."

"True…" On his feet, he cast his most handsome grin on first her, then the baby. "She's zonked. Must be nice, doing nothing with your days but sampling boobies then napping."

"Heath!" Libby couldn't help but laugh. "I'm glad your mom wasn't around to hear that."

"You'd think by now she'd realize I'm no saint."

"Whatever. Ready to start on your push-ups?" Because if his six-pack abs weren't enough of a sight to behold, his backside was even better!

"I probably should." He kissed the baby on her forehead, then Libby full on the lips. It was a foregone conclusion that with each passing day she was falling more for him, but to what end? With both of them going their separate ways, officially moving forward didn't make sense. But then neither did anything in regard to her feelings for him. For now, her only plan was to enjoy what little time they had left and sort out the rest once he was gone.

From inside, the phone rang, the sound carrying clearly through the open windows.

"I'll get it," Heath volunteered.

Libby was all too happy to let him. Though she felt a thousand times better than she had before giving birth, she still lacked her former energy and felt as if she cat-napped almost as much as her baby!

A few minutes later Heath emerged from the house, wearing the kind of scowl he'd once been famous for, but she thankfully hadn't seen in a while.

"What's wrong?"

"That was Hal on the phone."

"And?" She steeled herself for the next bit of bad news concerning her disaster of a vehicle.

"The last part came in yesterday, and today you are the proud owner of a vehicle that actually runs. Plus, he grabbed the last few parts for less than expected, so he's giving you a break on labor and only charging five hundred bucks."

"That's all? I mean, that's a lot, but I already have that much saved from my art show profits. I can't believe it." She grinned. "After all this time, it's finally done." But then reality set in. She'd planned on at least six more days with Heath. Who would've thought she'd be the one leaving ahead of him? "Guess I need to ask Doc Meadows if it's safe for Heather and me to travel."

"No. I think you need at least a couple months—maybe even more—to fully heal."

"Who made you a doctor?" And why did he care, considering he wasn't even going to be here?

"Lib, think about it. You're all the time drifting off. What if you fall asleep behind the wheel? It just doesn't seem safe for you to drive all that way on your own. Besides which, your car isn't exactly baby friendly—especially once you cram all your pottery gear in the back. Poor Heather's going to be crushed."

Libby loved that he was concerned, but he didn't exactly have a say in the matter. "Let's agree to disagree."

"What's there to disagree with? I'm right. End of story. Don't you have a doctor's appointment tomorrow? I'll bet even Doc Meadows tells you there's no way you can travel that far for a *long* time. You're talking a good seven hours, babe—without traffic. No. I don't want you going."

"Do you have any idea how crazy you sound? As much as I love kissing you, that's really all we share."

"How can you say that? We share Heather. I was there when she was born. You even gave her my name. No matter what, we'll always have that bond."

"True, but a bond is a lot different than a commitment, Heath. You have no more say over my life than I do yours. How would you feel if I said, nope, you can't leave for the navy so soon after I had the baby? I need you to stay here and help with late-night feedings."

"Is that how you feel?"

Yes! She was terrified of being a single mom, but figured she would eventually have to get used to it. Why prolong the inevitable? She'd always been a rip-the-bandage-off-quick kind of girl.

"No. I would never ask you to stop doing something important to you, and I'd appreciate you doing the same for me."

He sighed before dropping to the ground for his push-ups. "We'll talk about it later. Mind timing me?"

"Yes, I mind timing you. Since you apparently control everything, do it yourself." Cradling Heather to her chest, Libby was off the swing and headed for the motel office to find Gretta. On her way, she dropped Heath's stupid stopwatch onto the soft grass near his stupid—albeit handsome—head.

"I DON'T MEAN to be nosy," Gretta said on the way to pick up Libby's car, "but were you and Heath arguing? I had all the windows open and could hear you from the front desk."

"I wouldn't call it arguing so much as having a difference of opinion." Since Heather's car-safety seat was installed in Gretta's SUV, it made sense to ask Heath's mom to drive her the five minutes to Hal's shop. As an added bonus, she was able to get away from Gretta's son for at least a little while. Libby needed to not only cool down, but have time to think. She hated that Heath had made valid points. What would she do with all of her pottery supplies? Ship it to her parents? Store it here in town, then drive back down for it later? One thing she couldn't do now that she had a baby was pile it all in her car. "He thinks it's not safe for me or the baby to travel so soon."

Gretta shocked her by telling her to ignore her worrywart son. "You know, if you were still in rough shape or Heather had complications, I would agree, but you and the baby seem stronger every day. Heath was born three weeks before his father was being shipped out to Japan. Well, he thought I should stay in San Diego, but the whole reason I married a navy man—besides the fact that he made my heart flutter every time he smiled—was because I craved the adventure of that lifestyle. No way was I staying behind."

She pulled into Hal's lot, parking her vehicle beside Libby's. "I'm not saying it was easy, but I did it and was glad. If you feel compelled to finish your journey home,

I won't even lie about missing having you and the baby at the house, but I knew from the start that this was only a temporary layover for you."

Teary from Gretta's admissions, Libby unfastened her seat belt and leaned over to give her a hug. "You've been so amazing. Really. No matter what happens with my parents, I want to keep in touch."

"Absolutely." With a wince, she said, "I almost hate to ask, but what about Heath? Do you think you two will ever be more than friends with benefits?"

"Gretta!" Libby's cheeks superheated with mortification. Had she found out about their night in the pool?

"Oh, you know what I mean. I've seen you two kissing when you think no one's looking."

"It's complicated…." Libby would've liked nothing more than to tell Gretta that her long-term forecast with Heath looked sunny, but honestly? Nothing could be further from the truth.

Chapter Sixteen

The next morning, Heath still detected a chill from Libby, which was no doubt why he'd been relegated once again to being stuck in the clinic's waiting room.

Because of the whole car-seat issue, he'd driven Libby and the baby in his mom's SUV. Libby had wanted to transfer Heather's seat to her car, but to his way of thinking, the very idea was ludicrous. So much so that he'd called Hal to see about maybe making a few *arrangements*. Libby would be so excited when she found out what he'd done for her.

Hell, he was excited. He'd never pulled off this big of a surprise.

From behind her battle station, Eloise glared even more than usual. "Your mother told me you're leaving soon. Heading back to Virginia Beach?"

"Yes, ma'am."

"Good." Not even bothering to look his way, she carried on with her paperwork.

"Are you ever going to get over me picking your roses?"

She snorted. "Oh—I was over that a long time ago. Now I just don't like the way you're toying with Libby's affections."

There were about a half dozen verbal grenades Heath would've loved to toss her way, but instead he focused more intently on the teenage heartthrob edition of *People*.

"Is this a new top secret SEAL skill you're working on?"

"What's that?"

"Reading magazines upside down?"

"As a matter of fact, yes. So would you mind leaving me to my work?"

She just shook her head.

Annoyed by pretending he couldn't care less what was going on back in Libby's exam area, Heath tossed the magazine to a side table in favor of pacing out front.

What was taking so long?

Could something be wrong with Libby or the baby?

Should he storm her exam room to check for himself? Just in case? He raked his hands through his hair that would need to be cut before heading back to base.

Libby made him feel perilously close to losing his sanity. And he never would have expected to fall so completely for a long-lashed, blue-eyed vixen who barely weighed over six pounds! He loved everything about Heather, from her tiny fingers and toes, to the adorable sucking sounds she made when she slept, to her impossibly sweet smell when she was fresh from her bath.

He didn't want to admit what the sight of Libby breastfeeding her did to him.

He hadn't meant to go all caveman on her the previous morning when they'd found out about her car, but this was uncharted territory for him. Sure, he'd heard his friends talk about how they felt when they had kids, but he hadn't really understood until he'd experienced it himself.

True. Only one problem, his conscience was all too kind to point out. *Heather's not your kid, any more than her mother's your girl.*

That sobering thought sent him jogging around the lot.

Fifteen minutes later, Libby finally exited the clinic with Heather's cumbersome carrier in her hands.

"Well?" He jogged to her, taking the baby. "You were in there forever. Everything okay?"

"Yes. Why wouldn't it be? In fact, the doctor said as long as I have plenty of rest before the drive, he didn't see any reason why I couldn't leave tomorrow."

That soon? No. No way was Heath ready to give either of them up just yet. Trouble was, her leaving wasn't his call.

"ARE YOU SURE you don't want to wait until Sunday to go?" Gretta asked. She held napping Heather to her chest as they sat out by the pool. They'd just eaten turkey sandwiches Morris had brought from the diner. "That way you can have a little extra time with Heath. See him off with me that morning at the airport. Lord knows I could use the moral support."

"I'm sorry...." Libby swallowed the lump in her throat with a sip of iced tea. After all Gretta had done for her, Libby felt awful making her say goodbye to her son on her own, or with just Morris. But she knew there was no way she could watch Heath leave for his flight's gate without losing it. No. She'd be better off leaving first. That way she wouldn't be tempted to beg him to take her and Heather with him. She'd already sold enough pieces in Zoe's gallery to prove to herself she could make it on her own. But did she want to? What was the point when sharing Heather with Heath would mean so much more? "I wish…I were strong enough, but I'm not…."

Gretta placed her free hand over Libby's. "I'm sorry, too. For all practical purposes, Heath's been lost to me since Patricia's been gone. But you changed everything— for all of us. You brought him back to life, and for that I'll forever be grateful. But I've spun this fantasy about you two becoming more to each other, and that wasn't fair to either of you. For that, I'm sorry."

Libby shrugged. "No need to apologize. Heath's a good man. Any woman would be lucky to have him."

"Just not you?"

HEATH'S MOM HAD wanted to throw a party for Libby's last night in town, but Heath had nixed that idea. Selfishly, he wanted Libby all to himself when he presented his surprise.

He couldn't wait to see her smile. This was gonna be big. *Huge.* He'd blow her mind with how much he cared for not only her, but tiny Heather.

With Gretta safely off at her Friday night, all-girl poker game, and his uncle busy at the diner, the moment had finally come for Heath to make his presentation.

"Lib?" he called from the kitchen.

"Yeah?" she answered from the bedroom.

"Could you please come here for a minute?" Excitement had his heart racing.

"I'm busy. With Heather finally full and napping, I've got to pack all of my stuff to store in the shed. Your mom said she wouldn't mind me stashing it there until I get settled."

"Okay, well, I'll be happy to help you finish if you'd just help me for a sec."

Sighing, she left her room. One hand fisted on her hip, the other holding the baby monitor, her hair piled into a glorious mess of curls atop her head and her full lips pressed into a frown, she for sure didn't have a clue what was coming. "Okay, I'm here. Where's the fire?"

"Outside. But first, you're going to need to put this on." He took a red bandana from his back pocket, waving it like a flag.

"Put it where? And why?"

"Like a blindfold. Here, I'll put it on for you." She wasn't making this easy. In fact, since he'd told her he didn't want her leaving, nothing between them had felt easy or *right*. He hated her running off to Seattle with the gaping rift between them, but as soon as she saw her surprise, any awkwardness would be behind them. He was sure of it.

"Heath…" Her voice warned of a pending explosion. "You and your mom didn't plan something nutty like a surprise party, did you? Because—"

"Relax. Mom wanted to, but I shut her down. This surprise is a simple gift from me to you."

Libby's heart galloped. "I don't know about this…."

"Trust me. Take my hand and just trust me that this will make you deliriously happy—at least I hope so."

Mind racing with the forbidden, slightly kinky thrill produced by the blindfold, Libby's mouth went dry while other parts of her grew damp.

Alone in her room, with Heather fast asleep in the antique oak cradle that had once been Heath's, she'd focused on packing to keep her mind from straying to how much she'd miss Gretta and Morris. Fred and Sam. Even Hal and his sons. But the one person she'd miss the most was Heath. His sexy smile and haunting pale green eyes. His laugh and especially his kisses.

She'd never seen him downright playful like this. Could he be on the verge of proposing? No. No way. But what if he was? What would she say? Would she and Heather go with him to his base right away, or wait until they were married? She put a stop to the thoughts rambling in her head, driving her mad. Most days, he seemed more enthralled with her baby than her.

"Just a little farther," he coaxed, when the screen door creaked behind them. "Watch out for the uneven brick...."

Having temporarily lost her sense of sight, his voice alone both carried and thrilled her. She tried not to get too excited by the hope in her heart and what she thought his gift might be.

"Ready?" He held her safe by bracing his hands on her shoulders.

She nodded. "I should take off my blindfold?"

"Yes, ma'am."

Excitement turned her knees to mush. Hands trembling, she inched the bandana back, wanting to prolong the delicious anticipation and thrill soon to follow.

"Aw, come on," he teased, taking the baby monitor. "You're killing me. You've gotta go faster than that."

She tugged it the rest of the way off, then brushed flyaway curls from her eyes before thrill turned to confusion.

Alongside his old truck, parked where her Bug used to be hulked a massive, candy apple–red SUV.

"Well?" Heath moved to the car, giving the rear side panel a Vanna White flourish. "Isn't she a beauty?"

"I don't understand...." Was her ring inside?

"It's yours. Well—like not officially, until you sign over the title for your Bug, but I got you a sweet trade-in deal, then paid cash for the rest, so you're all set. Plus, since you're artsy, I figured you'd like the bright color, right?"

"Wait, what?" So the surprise she'd stupidly, naively, insanely thought would be a proposal was this? "Without even asking, you sold my car? The first car I could afford with my very own money."

"Well, yeah." He opened the rear cargo door with additional flair. "Look at all this space. Not only will Heather's gear fit, but your pottery wheel and kiln. Plus, this has the highest safety rating in its class—airbags everywhere—but not the kind that could suffocate the baby. I checked."

With him beaming as if he'd just presented her with the crown jewels, Libby couldn't very well yell at him. *But he sold my car!*

Deep down, and infinitely more upsetting, her disappointment had nothing to do with her car. His grand surprise hadn't been an engagement ring. His gesture was generous, kind and thoughtful. By far the nicest thing anyone had ever in her wildest dreams done for her. But it wasn't a declaration of love.

"What's wrong? If the color's not right, the dealer said we can have another model down from Portland in a day."

Tears started and wouldn't stop. Turning away from him, she dashed for the back porch.

"Babe?" Jogging after her, he asked, "Talk to me. I expected you to be thrilled."

She flung herself onto the wicker love seat where Gretta sat in the mornings to do the newspaper's crossword.

"What's wrong?" He perched alongside her, tugging

her into his arms, against his chest, overwhelming her with the special masculine scent that was uniquely his. A scent she was likely never going to enjoy again. But what had she expected? She'd set herself up for this catastrophe by always looking at her glass not just half-full, but bubbling over.

"Say something—anything. I'm dying here."

"G-good," she sniffled, "because I am, too. Thank you, but I can't accept your gift, Heath. It's too much." It was the kind of thing a guy presented to his wife. The mother of *his* child. Not a random stranger he'd plucked from the road.

"You're being ridiculous. Of course you're taking the car. It's a safety issue. I'm already going to miss you and the baby like crazy. But I'll seriously never be able to do my job if I'm constantly worrying about you and Heather rolling around in that sardine can on wheels."

"Thanks for that," she said with a half laugh, "but I'm still not taking it. You'll have to get my old car back."

"Is this a pride thing? Like when you first got to town and never wanted my help? If so, you need to get over it. Put Heather first. Just like you probably should've called your parents for help a long time ago. Pride can be a bitch. You're damn lucky you ended up with me and my mom instead of some psycho serial killer."

"Oh—if you want to take this conversation to the gutter, hon, let's go." Standing, because she couldn't bear a moment's more of her bare thigh touching his, she placed her hands on her hips. "You wanna know why I'm really so upset? It has nothing to do with the car. I'll concede to you that as a newborn's parent, it's probably time to give up my old ride. But what're you giving up, Heath? If you're so concerned about not only missing me, but worrying about my safety and Heather's, then why not take us with you? The real reason I don't want that shiny new car? It's because I'd set my every hope and dream on you presenting me with an engagement ring. It could've been a bread tie for all I cared, I just want to be with you. I want to raise Heather with you. Which is stupid, right? Considering we've only been on one official date, and even that wasn't so much a formal affair, but more of an excuse to get out the house."

There. She'd said it. Admitted just how much she'd come to care for him. And what did he do? Absolutely nothing other than lean forward, covering his face with his hands.

Classic Heath. Totally avoiding the issue.

His silence was crushing.

The ache in her chest was unbearable.

What had she done? She never should've set her cards out on the table, but instead, kept them close, where no one—especially him—would ever see.

Finally, he stood, rammed his hands in his cargo pants pockets. "Your car was already sold to a collector, so there's no getting it back. Mom's a notary, so when she gets done tonight, you'll need to sign off on the old title, which I found in your glove box—not a safe place for it, by the way—and the new one. The keys are in the ignition. There's also what I hope is enough cash for gas money and food and tags once you get to Seattle. I already paid the tax. Sorry I went behind your back, but it is for your own good—and the baby's. Despite what you think, I care about you both—deeply. But marriage?" He drove the rejection knife deeper with a short laugh and shake of his head. "That's something I just can't do."

Chapter Seventeen

Rather than face Libby in the morning, Heath grabbed Sam and spent the night at his cabin.

He woke to thick fog.

It reminded him of the day he'd encountered Libby on the highway, and of the myriad changes that had occurred in him ever since.

Memories of their brief time together accosted him, making the pain of letting her go all the more acute. He recalled chopping wood, glancing up to see her standing on his front porch, curls a tousled mess with his favorite blanket wrapped around her. It had smelled of her floral-fruity sweetness for days. There was her finding Sam, and then him acting like an ass for no better reason than she'd altered his status quo. He saw her sitting at her pottery wheel, looking sexy covered in slick clay. Laughing around the dinner table with his mom and uncle and Mason and Hattie. Spoiling his dog. That wild night in the pool he'd tried a hundred times to pretend hadn't mattered as much as it did. Her yelling at him to get back to work, to life, to never forget Patricia but to also never forget to live.

Memories hit faster and harder, culminating in those precious few moments after Heather's birth. How lucky and blessed had he been to bear witness to such an intimate moment. Inviting him in had been such a gift. Yet now, he was essentially throwing her away—Heather, too.

Why? What was he so afraid of?

Sitting on the wooden porch steps, listening to Sam's bark echo through woods, Heath realized he didn't have a clue what he was afraid of, just that he was. He wished he could offer Libby marriage. With everything in him, he wholly believed she deserved her happily ever after. But was he really the guy who could deliver?

Not even close.

"If you'll stay a few minutes longer," Gretta urged Libby at 6:00 a.m., "I'm sure Heath will be here for a proper goodbye."

"No, he won't." Libby had cried so much after he'd left the previous night that she had no tears left. It didn't matter if he showed up, because at this point, they had nothing to say.

"But I don't understand...." Gretta looked to the car, then back to Libby, no doubt noticing her tearstained cheeks and bloodshot eyes. "Are you sure you're even all right to drive?"

"I'm good." She crushed Gretta in a hug. "How do I begin to thank you? You literally saved my life."

"Since you saved my son's, consider us even. Although, this sure isn't ending the way I envisioned. When he told me about this car, I assumed he bought it with the express intention of you and Heather driving east to join him. It'd make a perfect family car. Plenty of room for even more gorgeous babies."

True. Which made how they'd left things all the more depressing.

The SUV was over-the-top sumptuous with heated leather seats, a sunroof, built-in DVD players in the seat backs and OnStar complete with a one-year service contract. Who did that? How could Heath claim to feel nothing for her, yet pay cash to buy her a vehicle that must've cost more than she'd made the whole previous year?

Heath had already installed Heather's safety seat, and Libby had to admit, even the new car smell made her feel good about slipping the baby inside.

"I guess now that Heather's settled, I'm good to go." True to Heath's word, all of her pottery equipment fit neatly inside, meaning she hadn't even needed to take Gretta up on her offer for storage. Another sobering thought, considering she'd looked forward to at least having an excuse to visit Heath's mom and uncle again.

Morris jogged over from the diner. "Good! Glad to see I'm not too late." He handed her a bulging white paper take-out bag. "Here's a little something for your trip. A couple of those turkey sandwiches you like, cookies, chips and a few bottles of water. Hopefully, that'll tide you over."

"You're such a sweetheart." Throat tight, she hugged him, as well. "Thanks so much—for everything."

"It's been my pleasure. Come back anytime."

Unable to speak, she nodded, ambushed them both with more hugs, then climbed behind the wheel of her new car, apprehensive of what the next chapter in her life would bring.

"IF YOU WEREN'T taller than me, I'd turn you over my knee."

"Mom, please give it a rest." Heath had checked his duffel and been given his boarding pass. Now all that remained was saying goodbye with a promise to at least try to be home for Thanksgiving. "I know you spun this fantasy of Libby and me ending up together, but it wasn't meant to be."

After a sarcastic snort, she crossed her arms. "Not meant to be, or you're just too scared to love again?"

Her words cut to his core. Of course, she was right, but he'd be damned if he'd admit it.

"Please, Mom, leave it alone. I gave Libby a pretty awesome parting gift, so—"

"Wait—" she laughed "—that car was your attempt to bribe her into forgiving you for not wanting to take things further?"

"Do we have to do this now?"

"Not at all." On her tiptoes, she kissed his cheek. "You'd just better make darned sure you come home safe, so when we have more time together, I can knock some sense into you."

"Yes, ma'am. And thanks again for watching Sam. I appreciate it."

"Since that dog is the only grandson I'm likely to have, did I really have a choice?"

"Ha-ha." He hugged her for all he was worth, kissed the crown of her head then launched his official fresh start, praying it was better than the possibility of a future with Libby and Heather that he'd just left behind.

"Miss Libertina! You're home—*with a baby*." Olga, the housekeeper who had been with Libby's family since Libby had been a little girl, made the sign of the cross on her chest. "I'll go get your mother."

Just like that, Libby was left on her own in the white marble-floored entry hall. Though it had been five years since she'd been home, nothing had changed. The double staircase still looked imposing and the compass rose table still held a towering fresh floral arrangement that was no doubt still replaced every four days. The cloying rose scent did nothing to calm her upset tummy.

She hadn't been called by her given name of Libertina since she'd left. It was her great-grandmother's. Libby had always found it a comfort that her namesake had been a bit of a rebel—driving her own car, cavorting without a proper chaperone and even wearing makeup! The thought of these supposed horrors made Libby smile.

Cradling Heather closer, she drew strength from her baby's sweet scent. "How much easier would our lives had been if Heath had taken us with him?"

Easy, yes, but a solution to finally heal the rift in her own family? No. For her daughter's sake—for her own— she needed this reunion. Whatever the outcome may be.

"It's true. You're really here…." Her mother ran— something Rose Dewitt never did off of a treadmill or personal training session—to embrace her daughter. Her tears crushed Libby, making her all at once guilty and sorry and ashamed for causing her mother pain. "I was so afraid we'd never see you again. And who's this?" she asked, cupping her flawlessly manicured hand to Heather's cheek. "She's beautiful."

"This is my daughter—Heather."

"And her father?"

Libby raised her chin. "Is long gone."

"I see. May I?" She held out her arms to hold the baby.

Libby transferred her sleeping child to her mom, whose eyes shone with tears.

"Thank you," her mom said.

"For what?"

"Trusting in us enough to come home. This is where you belong, and now that you're here, Daddy and I will find you the perfect husband—I'm sure he has loads of eligible bachelors at his firm. You might be a single mother now, but trust me, you won't have to bear that stigma for long."

The longer Rose spoke, the more Libby's stomach roiled. Now wasn't the time, but before her mom got too carried away, she needed to know Libby had no interest in a marriage of convenience. She'd had nearly nine, long months to adjust to being a single mom, and though she knew it would be tough, she was no longer afraid.

Yes, her life would've been more fun with Heath, but just because he'd rejected her didn't mean she planned on shutting down.

Her mother fingered Libby's long, pale curls. "First thing in the morning, we'll take you to my stylist to tame your hair. From there, you'll need clothes and a facial and nails—but listen to me. I'm getting ahead of myself. Of course, first, we should find your father. I know he'll be just as pleased you're home as I am."

I wouldn't be so sure.

"It's about damn time you got home!" Heath's longtime friend and fellow SEAL team member, Deacon Murphy, slapped him a high five. "Man, am I glad to see you."

"Likewise." Heath accepted the longneck beer his friend offered.

The guys had all gotten together Sunday night for beers and a beach bonfire.

Right after he'd unloaded his gear in the three-bedroom apartment he'd share with the only two other single guys on the team, "Cowboy" Cooper Hansen and "Dodger"

Clay Monroe, they'd loaded him into Cooper's truck to haul Heath to the beach that had once felt like his second home.

His mind had a tough time wrapping around the fact that he'd started his day on the Pacific and ended up on the Atlantic. Regardless, water was water and the crashing surf and briny tang both comforted and gave him strength.

It had been on this very beach that he'd proposed to Patricia, yet all he could think about was Libby. How she was doing with her folks and whether or not they were as accepting of her being a single mom as he and his family had been.

"HELLO, DADDY." LIBBY'S FATHER, Winston, Seattle's former mayor who now ran his own law firm, sat at the head of the dining room table looking every bit as imposing as he had back when he'd ruled the city.

"Libertina..." Though he'd never been an overly demonstrative man, he rose, circling the table to hold her, lightly rocking her back and forth.

Relief and love for this man whom she'd alternately hated and adored flowed through her like a healing balm. The years and harsh words that had spanned between them faded, leaving only love.

"I'm sorry." He gripped the back of one of the ornately carved chairs. "I—I made a lot of mistakes. Namely, putting my need for reelection ahead of you—your feelings. Forgive me?"

"Of course." Could it truly be this easy? Erasing years of confusion and pain? She had a hard time believing it would. A long time ago, she'd stopped trusting her father.

He'd turned on her at a time when she'd never needed his guidance more.

Now here she was again, needing his emotional support, which he oddly enough seemed willing to give. But at what cost?

BY OCTOBER, HEATH and his team had performed a pair of in-and-out covert ops in Syria and a two-week stint in Afghanistan. His body was rock hard and once again accustomed to constant abuse. His mind was sharp and senses honed.

As for his heart—it ached.

Now he hurt almost as badly as he had when Patricia died. But he hadn't *lost* Libby. Instead he'd been too cowardly to even try for something deeper. He couldn't stop wondering what would happen to him if he did go all-in, and then something happened to her, too. Or, God forbid, something happened to Heather? He wasn't sure he was capable of surviving another loss on that scale.

A little past seven on Halloween, he pulled his truck up to the curb at Mason and Hattie's new place. The two-story brick colonial sat in a quiet Norfolk neighborhood that was all decked out for the holiday with orange lights strung on white picket fences and hay bales, scarecrows and mums decorating every front porch.

Ghosts, witches, vampires and fairies roamed the streets in all directions, making him wish he'd stayed back at the apartment, nursing a few beers and playing "Call of Duty."

He didn't have to ring the bell as he damn near got run down by a gang of Power Rangers on sugar highs.

"Glad you could make it," Mason said. "Especially

since you're my excuse for turning this gig over to Hat Trick and Pandora."

"Good call." The last thing Heath needed was to be reminded of a holiday that was predominantly for kids. Had Libby bought Heather one of those little baby costumes he'd seen the infant crowd wearing? If so, she had to be the cutest kid in the history of the holiday. The fact that he was missing out on sharing it with Libby and her, taking dozens of pics he could brag about Monday morning made him sick inside. But that longing still wasn't enough to override the fear.

"NICE MEETING YOU," Libby said in the entry hall on Halloween night to Drew Corbett—a junior partner at her father's firm. She'd wanted to get Heather one of the cute costumes she'd seen at the mall, but her mother had thought it would be déclassé. Instead, she'd opted for a taffeta dress in burnt orange with chocolate-toned tights and matching patent-leather Mary Janes. The only holiday concession her mother had sanctioned was a candy corn and silk flower headband. "My father's told me a lot about you."

"Likewise." He handed her a bouquet of yellow, orange and white mums. "Happy Halloween."

"Thank you." She repositioned the baby to her other arm. "Come on in. The party's this way...." Party being a relative term. This was hardly the kind of lively, the-more-the-merrier affair Gretta would've thrown. With aperitifs, champagne, a full bar and five-man jazz band, the night was by invitation only. Libby had quarreled with her mom about Heather even making an appearance, but surprisingly, her father served as her champion, explaining that Drew should see what he's getting into. The comment hadn't set well then, and still didn't now, but as was the case more and more, she swallowed her feelings to please her parents and keep the peace. "Hope you're hungry. Mom's caterer made enough to feed a small country."

"I'm always hungry," Drew said, following after her. "I run marathons."

"That's great."

"I think so. Running gives you quite a natural high. Do you? Run?"

She laughed. "I change diapers."

"Oh. Sure." The night only got worse from there.

By the time her "date" left, Libby had long since put Heather to bed and was headed that way herself when her parents called her into her father's mahogany-paneled office.

"You sure did shine tonight," her father said from behind his desk once she'd sat next to her mother in one of the leather chairs facing him. "I've never been more proud."

"I feel the same," her mother echoed.

Libby wished she found more joy in her parents' statements, but all she really felt was flat. A nanny had been hired for Heather, and Rose kept Libby so busy with hair and nail appointments, shopping and club lunches that she couldn't remember the last time she'd worked with her pottery wheel—not that it would've even been allowed in the house. She'd touched base with Zoe the previous week, and the gallery owner had all but begged her for more merchandise.

"You're probably wondering why I've got you in here so late." Winston sat taller in his leather desk chair.

"Yes." She hid a yawn behind a tight laugh.

Rose patted her knee. "Your father and I have wonderful news. You're going to be so pleased."

Had they refurbished the boathouse to serve as her art studio as she'd requested? For the first time since her arrival, they'd actually piqued her interest in what they had to say.

"You and Drew seemed to hit it off."

She shrugged. "He's okay."

"Well, since he's my sharpest junior partner, I'd hoped—of course in due time—you'd find him more than just *okay*."

While Libby sat shell-shocked, her mother prattled on.

"I've always had my heart set on a June garden wedding for you, but if that's too soon, maybe September? Or even Christmas. Your bouquet could be poinsettias mixed with white orchids."

Mortified didn't come close to describing the thick disappointment making her limbs and heart heavy. "You guys can't be serious?"

"Honey," her father said, "Drew's a wonderful man. Your mom and I have noticed how lonely you've seemed, and thought maybe a handsome new fella in your life might make you smile."

"Whoa." Libby stood and forced deep breaths to keep from saying something she'd later regret. For Heather's sake she wouldn't burn bridges, but enough was enough. "While I appreciate you both caring how I feel, please slow down. Ever since I came back, I've let you two dictate my every move. What I wear, eat. How I style my hair. Do you have any idea how long it took for me to grow it that long? It made me feel pretty.

"Now…" She touched her trembling hand to her shorn locks. She might have a sophisticated bob, but she didn't

feel like herself. "I feel like a robot, constantly following your commands."

"Sweetheart…" When Rose reached for her hand,
Libby stepped just out of reach.

"I love you two. I hoped coming back would change
things, but everything's the same. You don't want me to
grow into a self-sufficient adult, but keep me under a
glass dome. Like a doll that's for looking, not touching.
But that's not who I am. I hate these uptight clothes—"
she tugged the jacket of her Chanel suit "—and I miss
my work. Did you know my pottery now sells out of a
gallery? No, you don't, because you never asked and I
knew it'd only upset you if I told you. But how sick is
that? That I knew you wouldn't be happy learning that
I'm actually a working artist."

"Libertina, honey—" her mother went to her, tucking
Libby's hair neatly behind her ears "—calm down. Of
course we're proud of you. We just thought that with the
baby, you'd be too tired to work. I was exhausted after
having you. And if you don't care for Drew, your father
has lots of other men whose company you might enjoy."

On the heels of a near-hysterical laugh, she said, "My
name's *Libby*. And the last thing I want is another man.
Especially when there's someone I already care deeply
for."

"The baby's father?" Eyebrows raised, Rose cautiously
smiled. "You haven't told us much about him. What's he
like? By all means, invite him up for a weekend so we can
get to know him. Please, *Libby,* all we want is to see you
smile. We know we're not exactly part of the hip crowd,
but maybe we could be—if you'd meet us halfway?"

"Mom…" Libby was touched by her mother's speech,
but she wasn't sure what else to say. "This isn't about

you being *hip,* but letting me be me." Sighing, she cradled her forehead in her hands. "Maybe it'd be best for everyone if Heather and I just leave."

"And go where?" her father asked. "I promise I mean no disrespect by this, but, Libertina—Libby…" He smiled through silent tears that made Libby's heart ache. "The time you were gone was easily the darkest of my life. I may sound melodramatic with this next admission, but I honestly don't think I could survive if you left again—especially not taking my granddaughter with you. In light of that fact—" Fresh tears shined in his eyes as he looked to Libby's mom and then her. "If you promise to stay, and give your mother and I pointers on the proper etiquette of proud parents of an artist, I promise to never play matchmaker again—unless you want me to."

Her mother added, "And not only will I promise not to meddle in your love life, but leave you alone when it comes to your choice in hair and clothes. I'm sorry." Now, her mom was crying, too. "I thought I could make things the way they used to be, but what I never stopped to consider was that when you left, we weren't exactly functioning as a family, but more like a campaign machine."

"Mom…" Libby swiped tears of her own.

"Your mother's right." Her dad passed around a silver-plated tissue box, then took two for himself. "The way I treated you was deplorable. I can never apologize enough—to both of you. I put pride before family. Having you back, holding Heather…" He blew his nose. "With the benefit of hindsight, I realize you three ladies are my world. I love you."

Her parents weren't the demonstrative type, so when her dad stepped around his desk to give Libby a hug, then kiss her mom full on her lips, she couldn't be entirely sure she wasn't dreaming.

Gazing back to her daughter, taking Libby's hands in hers, her mother said, "If you stay, assuming you're okay with it, how would you feel about all of us transforming the boathouse into your ideal workspace? Whatever you need, sweetheart. Name it, and it's yours—even a second nursery so Heather can be with you while you work."

Libby crushed her mother and father in hugs. "I'd love that. I love you both so much." Through more tears, she added, "Daddy, I really am sorry for harming your campaign all those years ago. All I ever wanted was for you to love me for who I am—not who you *want* me to be."

"Done. Only…" Once she released him, he reached for his archaic Rolodex. "I do have contacts in the art world. I'll make some calls and then—"

"Winston!" her mother admonished. "Before you do anything regarding Libby's art career, don't you think it would be wise to first ask her?"

He reddened, but in a soft, uncharacteristically lovable way that prompted Libby to dive in for another hug.

Without Heath, Libby feared her life may never feel totally complete, but with her parents' emotional support, she'd just taken a giant step closer to finding happiness and that elusive sense of belonging she'd been looking for.

"THANKS FOR HAVING ME," Heath said to Hattie the Wednesday before Thanksgiving. His team had just finished debriefing from another run to Syria and he badly craved home cooking instead of the jar of mayo and pickles that were pretty much all he had in his fridge.

Mason was in the playroom reacquainting himself with his kids.

"Of course," Hattie said. "You know you're welcome anytime." After giving him the first decent hug he'd had in a long time, she asked, "How are your mom and uncle?"

"Good. Mom's relieved I'll be home for the holiday." While Hattie sprinkled crushed Corn Flakes atop her famous chicken casserole, he sat on a kitchen bar stool. "Truthfully, I'm shocked the CO gave me the time off. As long as I was gone, I was sure he'd keep me on lockdown."

She waved off his concern. "That's what the baby SEALs are for. You've earned your break."

"I guess. Got any beer?"

On her way to the fridge, she said, "That's a dumb question. Here."

"Bless you." He downed half the bottle.

After grabbing one for herself, she said, "I know this is no doubt the last thing you want to hear, but I got an email from Libby. She's doing well."

"Good for her. Glad one of us is."

He hated Hattie's wide-eyed look of concern.

"Don't even start. I'm honestly glad to be back at work. It's great being busy. Libby and I..." He finished his beer. "Got another?"

"Not unless you admit you two were more than friends."

"Let me get this straight—you're blackmailing me for beer?"

"Yep." She retrieved another cold one, wagging it in his face. "What're you gonna do about it?"

Sighing, he said, "You win. Had I stayed in Bent

Road, we'd probably still be together, but did you know she actually wanted to marry me?"

"Of course, I know." She grinned. "It was my idea."

"Are you kidding me? Why'd you go and tell her something like that? You know my history. I've already done the marriage routine, and there's no way I'm setting myself up for that kind of pain again should something go wrong."

"Yeah, but—" she popped the beer's twist-off cap and handed it to him "—what if you did marry her and the rest of your life went *really* right?"

Chapter Eighteen

Come morning, Heath rose extra early.

He stopped off at a grocery store for flowers, then drove through light drizzle toward Patricia's grave.

He needed to talk to her.

At 6:00 a.m., the lot was deserted. The groundskeeper waved Heath in upon opening the gate.

"How've you been?" Arthur asked. The hunched-over old guy had to be pushing ninety, but he always wore a smile. He lived in a small caretaker's house with his wife and a yappy little poodle that sometimes dug out from under his backyard fence and ran around peeing on graves. "Haven't seen you in a while."

"Some good days, some bad," Heath said. "How about you?"

"Happy wife, happy life." He knelt to fish an empty beer can from under an azalea. "Though this damp weather's got my arthritis acting up."

"Sorry to hear it."

"I'll be all right. By the time my Gladys adds a little whiskey to my coffee, then gives my shoulders a nice rub, I'll be A-okay."

Heath laughed. "Sounds good. I'll leave you to it."

He envied Arthur's seventy-year marriage. That was

the way it was supposed to be. That's the expectation he'd had when saying his vows.

With two hours to kill until he was due on base, Heath took his time winding through the graves. He liked looking at the really old ones, wondering about their lives. He was always surprised by how young people had been when they'd died in the 1800s. Patricia had also been stolen in her prime.

In front of her tombstone, he knelt, tearing out the few weeds before placing her flowers.

"Sorry it's been so long," he eventually said, "but you know how I never set much stock in these kinds of things. When you left me, I watched you go. Wherever you are, you're sure as hell not in this grave—at least not your spirit."

He sat back on his haunches, plucking more weeds and the too-long grass.

"Anyway, I've got a bit of a situation, and I don't know where else to turn. Everyone seems to think I should just jump right into another marriage, but..." He bent forward from the waist, pressing the heels of his hands against his stinging eyes. "It's not that easy, you know? I used to envy you for going first. I imagined you partying up there with angels, while I was stuck down here in hell. Only something happened this summer—I met someone. When we're together, she makes me feel like I could gladly go another fifty or so years.

"I'm pretty sure I really care about this woman, but not only do I feel guilty about leaving you behind, but what if she dies, too? It's scary—this whole relationship thing. I just wish you were here to tell me what to do."

Heath was so lost in his fear that he didn't notice the woman approaching until she was nearly on top of him.

"Good morning," she said. Her hair was blond—though not as pale as Libby's, and cut short. She pushed a stroller, and when he got a look inside, he saw an infant not much bigger than Heather was when she'd been born.

"Morning."

Just as soon as she'd appeared, she was gone, heading over a small hill.

But then a man appeared, chasing after the mother and child. Soon, he'd also vanished over the hill, leaving Heath once again alone.

All the times he'd visited Patricia's grave, he'd never seen anyone pushing a stroller.

"Was that supposed to be some kind of sign?" he asked. "Am I supposed to go after Libby, then bring her here? Home?"

He wasn't sure what he'd expected, but all he got was the familiar tightening in his chest from missing Libby and her baby. In that moment, he finally realized Patricia, his mom and Hattie had all been right—even Libby. They'd all told him, maybe not in the same words, that he couldn't spend the rest of his life with a grave.

Not only did he need Libby, but hopefully, she and her baby still needed him.

OVER THANKSGIVING WEEKEND, Heath started what he considered to be the toughest mission of his life when he flew to Portland for a brief bit of dicey—and expensive—business. He'd gotten Libby's snail mail address from Hattie, then programmed Libby's Seattle location into the map application on his phone.

After an excruciating five-hour trek in what felt like a tuna can of a car, he pulled into the circle drive of the largest home he'd ever seen. The damn thing looked like a mini White House—complete with a chandelier hanging from the portico's sheltered ceiling.

Whoa. He'd known Libby came from money, but nothing like this. Why hadn't he stopped for flowers or chocolates? For that matter, he didn't even have a ring. His sole focus had been on finding Libby, then apologizing for not having figured out how much he cared for her sooner.

After that, his plans pretty much depended on her reception.

He rang the bell.

It chimed with an elaborate, cathedral-like series of rings. From inside, he heard footsteps, and then the sound of someone opening a dead bolt.

"Yes?" a uniformed maid asked. "May I help you?"

He cleared his throat and stood taller. "I'm, ah, here to see Libby."

"Miss Libertina's no longer in residence."

Seriously? Libertina? And if she wasn't there, then where was she? "Do you know where she is?"

"One moment, please." Instead of inviting him inside, she shut the door in his face.

He glanced down at his desert fatigues and boots, wishing he'd thought to dress for the occasion. Could he have mucked this up any worse?

A good five minutes later, the door opened and an imposing man stepped out. Without even a courtesy greeting, he asked, "How much do you want?"

"E-excuse me?"

He held a leather-bound checkbook in one hand and a pen in the other. "You are my granddaughter's father, I take it? The one who broke my daughter's heart?"

"No, sir. I'm Heath Stone. Libby stayed with my mother and I when her car broke down."

"But she's driving a reasonably new car."

"Yessir, because I bought it. If she'd had her way by driving her old car, she'd have no doubt broken down again." As soon as the condemning words left his mouth, Heath felt disloyal for even saying them. This was the man who hadn't believed in her. As such, he didn't deserve to hear how amazing his daughter really was—even if she had argued with Heath regarding car safety.

"Then you're wanting reimbursement for that?"

Eyes narrowed, Heath said, "I don't mean to be disrespectful, but the only thing I want is your daughter. Is she here?"

Her father stared him down, giving Heath the sensation he was being appraised. "Yes and no."

"Okay…" For all the home's grandeur, the occupants were about as warm and fuzzy as a chunk of dry ice. "Which is it? Is she here or not? I really need to see her—and Heather."

The man's eyes narrowed. "What business do you have with my daughter?"

"With—or, even without—your permission, I plan to marry her."

LATE NOVEMBER DAYS didn't get much more beautiful than this. With the temperature in the high seventies and the sky streaked with orange and violet, Libby cradled Heather more snugly in her blanket, breathing deeply of the water's briny-rich smell.

Sam chased down the shore after a seagull.

"Doggy's silly, but we're lucky girls, aren't we? Have you ever seen a more gorgeous view?" Seated on the boathouse's newly installed swing, staring out at near-glassy Puget Sound, Libby almost felt whole.

Her parents had been wonderful in their support—more than she ever could've hoped for. The boathouse's lower floor now served as her studio and the upper floor was a posh one-bedroom apartment with a sumptuous nursery alcove. True to his word, Winston had stopped matchmaking and her mother joined all the right committees for the Seattle art scene.

Over the weekend, Libby and her parents and the baby had driven down to meet Heath's mother and uncle and even Zoe. The days had been idyllic. Libby cherished the time spent with everyone she loved—all save for one stubborn man she feared she may never get over.

She'd returned to Seattle with not only Sam, who'd been miserable cooped up with lazy Fred, but two gorgeous container gardens that had prompted her to make more until the deck surrounding her new home now made her heart sing from the dizzying array of colors and scents. Sweet snapdragons and petunias, pungent marigolds. Delicate lobelia and even robust tomato and pepper plants Hal had dug up for her from his vegetable garden.

Five more galleries had requested her work, and she'd even been invited to speak about her process at an upcoming showing. So many aspects of her life were incredibly satisfying, yet she'd be lying if she didn't admit to constantly missing Heath.

The sun took its sweet time setting, but that was okay. After a long day of spinning new projects, she was officially pooped, and all too happy to sit.

Just as the sky darkened, the faint sound of an engine alerted her to the fact that she soon wouldn't be alone. A service road made her home accessible for supply deliveries, but she wouldn't get one at this late hour.

"That's odd," she said to the baby. "Were you expecting a package?"

Heather gurgled and clapped her hands.

"That's what I thought."

Libby rose, assuming whoever drove the car was a lost tourist, and set Heather in the playpen she kept on the porch on sunny days, then crossed the pebbled parking area.

"Lose your way?" she asked the driver, who was exiting a VW Bug similar to the one she used to own. The resemblance was remarkable. It could've easily been her car—only better, as this one had been restored to its former glory.

"Yeah, I am lost," a dear, familiar voice said, "but not in the way you mean."

"Heath?" She didn't dare hope what his presence meant.

"I'm sorry." In four confident strides, he walked to her, wrapping his arms around her waist to lift her into a hug. She was still furious with him, but God help her, he was still the first one on her mind every morning and the last thing every night. Burying his face in her now shoulder-length hair, he breathed her in. "I'm so, so sorry. I messed up everything. Not telling you how I really felt. Selling your car. I was so afraid of losing you, I couldn't even conceive of keeping you."

"Keeping me?" she teased once he'd set her to her feet. "I'm not livestock." Smile fading, she added, "In all seriousness, you hurt me. I love you, Heath. I offered myself to you, and just like every other man in my life, you didn't want me."

"The hell I didn't. I'm pretty sure I've loved you from the first day we met, but I couldn't give myself permission to be with you. On so many levels, it felt wrong. But then, the more we were together, I couldn't get enough of you."

"And so you bought me a car that looks like my old one? Heath…" As lovely as the gesture was, she didn't want a car, but *him!*

"It's not a clone, but the real deal. I know it doesn't make up for the way I treated you, but what we shared scared me. You scared me."

"How?" She'd taken his hand, tracing the deep lines on his work-roughened palm. Dare she hope his being here meant he was prepared to at least try opening himself to another chance at love?

"You forced me to take stock of my life. You woke me from a deep sleep. For the longest time I didn't know what to do, or even how to act. But now I get it. I understand that loving you doesn't make what I shared with Patricia any less valid."

"Didn't I tell you that back in July?"

"What can I say?" When he kissed her, liquid heat coursed all the way to her toes. "I'm slow on the uptake, but now that I'm here, will you marry me? Oh—and if it make a difference, your dad even gave his consent."

"You asked my dad?" Her eyes widened.

"Well," he said, sheepishly smiling, "I sort of just told him. At the time, it seemed like the right thing to do."

"What did he say?"

"That he loves you. And more than anything, he wants you to be content. Does that make you happy?"

For once swallowing a knot in her throat caused by joyful tears, she nodded. "But not as happy as this…" She kissed him and kissed him until the sky turned dark and stars twinkled overhead.

Together, they played with Heather and made plans.

Sam returned from his latest adventure and bayed with excitement for a full five minutes upon discovering his former best buddy.

After Heather was fed and tucked into her cradle for the night, and Sam had fallen asleep in front of the crackling fire Heath built to ward off the chilly evening air, Libby and Heath shared a simple meal of scrambled eggs and toast much as they had the first day they'd met.

And then, finally, finally after months of yearning and hoping and praying and longing, Libby's body hummed with pleasure when Heath carried her to the bed, vowing to always love her in the most intimate way a SEAL can.

Epilogue

"Wait—you need something blue!" While Libby dashed off to find the racy blue garter she'd purchased for Gretta's wedding, Hattie and Pandora worked on the glowing bride's makeup and hair.

"I'm all of a sudden so nervous," Gretta said. "Libby, when you and Heath were married, did you feel this scared?"

Libby laughed. "Yes—but only because I was afraid the big lug might bolt. As tough as he was to catch, I wanted him officially mine as soon as possible. That's why we had a Christmas wedding."

"You were smart to not give him too much time to escape," Hattie said, with Pandora nodding in agreement.

"Gee, thanks guys." Hands on her hips, Libby shot her friends playful daggers.

"You know we're teasing."

The upstairs room had grown stuffy, so Libby opened the double doors leading to the veranda and the sweeping Puget Sound view. Since she and Heath were married, her parents had only grown more supportive. Libby and Heather often stayed with them when Heath was deployed. Not only had they purchased a Virginia Beach condo for east coast visits, but her mom had even gone so far as to offer their Seattle home for Gretta's June wedding. Rose was ecstatic to finally have a special occasion that called for raising a tent on the lawn.

A knock sounded on the bedroom door.

"Who is it?" Libby asked.

"Me," said a muffled male voice. "I wanna kiss my bride."

Gretta swiveled on her makeup chair. "Hal Kramer, you get away from that door this second or the wedding's off!"

"Not even one kiss?"

"No! It's horrible luck! Now, get!"

Fortunately for Gretta—and everyone else who'd shared in the planning—the ceremony went off without a hitch. The hundreds of pink roses and lilies were fragrant, the cake was beautiful and the dinner delicious.

"There you are," Heath said when Libby finally sat long enough to rest her swollen feet. At three months pregnant, overall, she still felt great, but knew the day was soon coming when she'd be huge and perpetually tired all over again. But it would be worth it—especially if her Norfolk obstetrician's suspicions came true. "I've missed you. Mom's been hogging you all to herself."

"I know. I'm sorry. Wanna dance?"

"Absolutely." Easing into his arms and resting her cheek against the muscled wall of his chest, Libby couldn't remember having ever felt more content.

Even Heather was giggly while Grandpa Winston waltzed her around the tent.

Turning introspective, Libby looked up at her handsome husband. "Do you ever regret all of this—*us?*"

"Are you kidding me?" Right in the middle of the dance floor, he thoroughly kissed her. "Even though combined we have more family and friends than we know what to do with, I wouldn't have it any other way."

"Good. I feel the same. Only, Heath?"

"Yeah?" When he looked down at her with his gorgeous, white-toothed grin, her heart never failed to flutter.

"How would you feel if I told you that during my last ultrasound—you know, the one when you were in Ghana—that the doctor told me he's pretty sure we're having triplets...?"

"How would I feel?" he asked, looking ecstatic but a bit dazed. "Like I might need a stiffer drink."

* * * * *

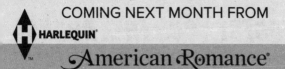

COMING NEXT MONTH FROM
HARLEQUIN
American Romance

Available July 1, 2014

#1505 THE REBEL COWBOY'S QUADRUPLETS
Bridesmaids Creek
by Tina Leonard

Cowboy Justin Morant is on the rodeo circuit looking for success—not a family. But when he meets Mackenzie Harper and her four baby girls, he realizes this may be the real gold buckle he's after!

#1506 THE TEXAN'S COWGIRL BRIDE
Texas Rodeo Barons
by Trish Milburn

Savannah Baron needs to find her mother, so she turns to P.I. Travis Shepard. During their search, Savannah and Travis grow closer, but falling in love was never part of the arrangement!

#1507 RUNAWAY LONE STAR BRIDE
McCabe Multiples
by Cathy Gillen Thacker

When Hart Sanders discovers he's a father, he wants to create a stable, loving home for his eighteen-month-old baby boy. But is turning to runaway bride Maggie McCabe the right thing...or will she run again?

#1508 MORE THAN A COWBOY
Reckless, Arizona
by Cathy McDavid

Liberty Beckett and Deacon McCrea have a chance for a serious relationship...but how can they take it when Deacon agrees to represent Liberty's father in a fierce legal battle that divides the entire Beckett family?

YOU CAN FIND MORE INFORMATION ON UPCOMING HARLEQUIN® TITLES, FREE EXCERPTS AND MORE AT WWW.HARLEQUIN.COM.

HARCNM0614

REQUEST YOUR FREE BOOKS!
2 FREE NOVELS PLUS 2 FREE GIFTS!

 HARLEQUIN

 American ★ Romance®

LOVE, HOME & HAPPINESS

YES! Please send me 2 FREE Harlequin® American Romance® novels and my 2 FREE gifts (gifts are worth about $10). After receiving them, if I don't wish to receive any more books, I can return the shipping statement marked "cancel." If I don't cancel, I will receive 4 brand-new novels every month and be billed just $4.74 per book in the U.S. or $5.24 per book in Canada. That's a savings of at least 14% off the cover price! It's quite a bargain! Shipping and handling is just 50¢ per book in the U.S. and 75¢ per book in Canada.* I understand that accepting the 2 free books and gifts places me under no obligation to buy anything. I can always return a shipment and cancel at any time. Even if I never buy another book, the two free books and gifts are mine to keep forever.

154/354 HDN F4YN

Name	(PLEASE PRINT)	
Address		Apt. #
City	State/Prov.	Zip/Postal Code

Signature (if under 18, a parent or guardian must sign)

Mail to the Harlequin® Reader Service:
IN U.S.A.: P.O. Box 1867, Buffalo, NY 14240-1867
IN CANADA: P.O. Box 609, Fort Erie, Ontario L2A 5X3

Want to try two free books from another line?
Call 1-800-873-8635 or visit www.ReaderService.com.

* Terms and prices subject to change without notice. Prices do not include applicable taxes. Sales tax applicable in N.Y. Canadian residents will be charged applicable taxes. Offer not valid in Quebec. This offer is limited to one order per household. Not valid for current subscribers to Harlequin American Romance books. All orders subject to credit approval. Credit or debit balances in a customer's account(s) may be offset by any other outstanding balance owed by or to the customer. Please allow 4 to 6 weeks for delivery. Offer available while quantities last.

Your Privacy—The Harlequin® Reader Service is committed to protecting your privacy. Our Privacy Policy is available online at www.ReaderService.com or upon request from the Harlequin Reader Service.

We make a portion of our mailing list available to reputable third parties that offer products we believe may interest you. If you prefer that we not exchange your name with third parties, or if you wish to clarify or modify your communication preferences, please visit us at www.ReaderService.com/consumerschoice or write to us at Harlequin Reader Service Preference Service, P.O. Box 9062, Buffalo, NY 14269. Include your complete name and address.

HARI3R

"Can I help you?"

"I'm looking for Mackenzie Hawthorne. My name's Justin Morant."

"I'm Mackenzie."

Pink lips smiled at him, brown eyes sparkled, and he drew back a little, astonished by how darling she was smiling at him like that. Like he was some kind of hero who'd just rolled up on his white steed.

And damn, he was driving a white truck.

Which was kind of funny, if you appreciated irony, and right now, he felt like he was living it.

Sudden baby wails caught his attention, and hers, too.

"Come on in," she said. "You'll have to excuse me for just a moment. But make yourself at home in the kitchen. There's tea on the counter, and Mrs. Harper's put together a lovely chicken salad. After I feed the babies, we can talk about what kind of work you're looking for."

The tiny brunette disappeared, allowing him a better look at blue jeans that accentuated her curves.

Damn Ty for pulling this prank on him. His buddy was probably laughing his fool ass off right about now, knowing how Justin felt about settling down and family ties in general. Justin was a loner, at least in spirit. He had lots of friends on the circuit, and he was from a huge family. He had three brothers, all as independent as he was, except for J.T., who liked to stay close to the family and the neighborhood he'd grown up in.

Justin was going to continue to ride alone.

Mrs. Harper smiled at him as he took a barstool at the wide kitchen island. "Welcome, Justin."

"Thank you," he replied, not about to let himself feel welcome. He needed to get out of here as fast as possible. This place was a honey trap of food and good intentions.

He needed a job, but not this job. And the last thing he wanted to do was work for a woman with soft doe eyes and a place that was teetering on becoming unmanageable. From the little he'd seen, there was a lot to do. He had a bum knee and a bad feeling about this, and no desire to be around children.

On the other hand, it couldn't hurt to help out for a week, maybe two, tops. Could it?

Look for THE REBEL COWBOY'S QUADRUPLETS,
the first story in the BRIDESMAIDS CREEK miniseries
by USA TODAY bestselling author Tina Leonard, from
Harlequin® American Romance®.
Available July 2014, wherever books and ebooks are sold.

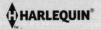
HARLEQUIN®

American Romance®

Love or family loyalty?

Liberty Beckett was so used to watching longtime crush
Deacon McCrea ride at her family's Reckless, Arizona, arena,
she nearly forgot the handsome cowboy was an attorney.
But it won't be hard to remember now that Deacon is
representing Liberty's father in the legal battle dividing the
Beckett clan and threatening the Easy Money Rodeo Arena.

This case is Deacon's chance to clear his name in Reckless.
He didn't anticipate the powerful effect Liberty would have
on him. Their attraction is undeniable…and a huge conflict
of interest. To save his career and Liberty's relationship with
her family, Deacon knows he needs to avoid Liberty.
But what a man needs and what he wants are two very
different things….

Look for
More Than a Cowboy
by *New York Times* bestselling author
CATHY MCDAVID,
the first title in the
Reckless, Arizona miniseries.

Available July 2014 from Harlequin® American Romance®.

HAR75529